Fantasy Island:

Carl Weber Presents

Fantasy Island:

Carl Weber Presents

Pyrple

www.urbanbooks.net

Urban Books, LLC
300 Farmingdale Road, NY-Route 109
Farmingdale, NY 11735

Fantasy Island: Carl Weber Presents

ISBN 13: 978-1-64556-550-5

First Mass Market Printing March 2024
First Trade Paperback Printing September 2023
Printed in the United States of America

10 9 8 7 6 5 4 3 2 1

Distributed by Kensington Publishing Corp.
Submit Orders to:
Customer Service
400 Hahn Road
Westminster, MD 21157-4627
Phone: 1-800-733-3000
Fax: 1-800-659-2436

Part One

He was lying. . . .

Chapter 1

Imani

The feel of his succulent lips brushed against my dark areola, sending chills from the roots of my hair to the cuticles of my toes. My arms wrapped around his strong back as he thrust powerfully into my love canal. The air was filled with a sound very similar to macaroni and cheese being stirred. My moans were loud, but so were his as we untidied what had once been a tidy bed.

"Imani."

His whisper in my ear alone was enough to send me to the edge of my orgasm. I held it at bay, knowing that once I released, he would too. But it was right there, just begging to come out and make me feel better than I had in a month.

"Imani?"

"Wait, I can't yet," I told him.

"You can't what?"

Wait. My lover's voice had changed. Not only did it change, but it was one I recognized. Suddenly I felt a hand on my shoulder, and I blinked out of my daydream. No longer was I in my comfortable bed. Instead, I was seated at a table inside of my favorite brunch spot staring into the confused face of my husband, Kevin. Standing near the table, holding the check for our food, was the very same man I'd been daydreaming about. The sexy young waiter looked to be in his mid-twenties, maybe 25. He was a decade younger than me, but old enough to evoke an unwarranted lust inside of me. I was a sucker for his chocolatey skin tone and full lips. My fingers truly felt as though they'd massaged the back of his tapered fade, and my body felt as if it really knew the weight of his. Kevin raised his brow at me and pointed at my stomach. It was then that I realized I was clutching it with one of my hands.

"You need to go to the bathroom, babe?" he asked.

"No!" I cleared my throat and sat up straight. "No, I, uhh, I'm fine. I think I just had one too many mimosas. Is it time to go?"

"Yeah, I was trying to get your attention, but you were zoned out. Alex here"—Kevin paused and pointed at the server—"just brought over the check, and I just realized I left my wallet on the dresser. I must have been rushing."

"No worries. I'll get it," I said and reached into my Louis Vuitton.

"You sure?"

"Well, unless you want to be in the back doing dishes, I don't have a choice. Here you go. Keep the change." I handed Alex a crisp $100 bill.

"Oh, wow. Thank you, ma'am. You two have a lovely day."

I gave a fake smile as Kevin and I got up and left the restaurant. As always, he held every door for me, a gesture that used to give me butterflies. But now it didn't do much for me. And it might have had something to do with the fact that it seemed to be *all* he did lately. After I was safely in his Corvette, I fought with myself to not say anything as he was walking around the back of the car. I smoothed my dress down over my thick thighs and told myself to let it go. However, in my thirty-five years of life, holding my tongue had never been my strong point. To me there was no great good in holding back the things I needed to say. All that ever did was babysit someone else's feelings, and that was something I never cared to do. *Especially* when I was a person in the equation. When he got in the car and drove away from the restaurant, I turned in my seat to face him.

"That's the third time in a month that you left your wallet at home when we went out some-where."

"Yeah, so? I'm forgetful sometimes." He shrugged like it was no big deal.

"I've never known you to be this forgetful. I guess I just want to make sure everything is all right on your end."

When Kevin and I got married, we made the decision to keep separate bank accounts. The one we shared was only used to deposit money so that our bills could be taken out. But it seemed as though recently it was I who was putting more money in that account to cover all of our necessities. It wasn't something we'd talked about, because when we first moved to L.A. it was I who was short, and Kevin covered for me. However, *I* was short because I hadn't yet found a storefront for my growing clothing line. That was also years ago though. Kevin, on the other hand, was the VP of an industrial company and made good money, a lot of it, too. Which was why I couldn't understand what was going on with him.

"Listen, next time I'll be sure to bring my wallet, okay? It's not that big of a deal."

He said it so casually. There was no hint of concern on his face even though I pointed out the other times he'd done the same thing. The way he was trying to brush me off was the reason I had to keep going.

"It *is* a big deal, especially when you came up short on the mortgage last month. And the month before that, I had to cover your car note for this toy *and* your Rolls-Royce! That doesn't include my cars."

"I thought we were a team, Imani." Kevin sighed and shook his head. "Because I quite vividly remember us moving here to L.A. to chase your dreams of being a fashion designer. I believe that was *after* you quit your high-paying job at the law firm. I paid for everything, *everything,* for two years so you could put everything you had into your business. Do you remember that?"

"Yes," I said and gave an eye roll.

"Okay then. All I'm asking you to do is support your man without questioning me. I love you."

I hated when he did that. Telling me he loved me before I was finished speaking was the ultimate silencer in our relationship. Once he said it, there was no getting through to him and the conversation at hand was over. We were almost to our Beverly Hills home when his phone began to ring from inside of the car's cup holder. I watched him grab it, look at the screen, and drop the phone in his lap. It was odd because Kevin never ignored calls, even when his mother rang a thousand times a day. If he wasn't busy, he would answer.

"Who was that?" I asked.

"I didn't recognize the number," he answered and rubbed his hand down his chin.

He was lying. See, Kevin had a tell whenever he wasn't being truthful, and that hand gesture was it. I figured that out soon after I started dating him after college. He wouldn't lie about anything big, just little white lies. I picked up on it and never told him that he had a tell. That way he wouldn't fix it. And that decision served me well in that moment and had me wondering who in the hell it was calling his phone.

"Mhm," was all I said.

When we arrived home, I kicked off my heels at the door as soon as I walked in. Kevin was right behind me, and we made our way up the spiral staircase. The banister tickled the palm of my hand, and it was then that I realized the effects the four mimosas I drank had on me. I didn't stumble up the steps. I felt like I was floating. Not only that, but my clit hadn't stopped thumping since my daydream at the restaurant, and I was hornier than ever.

When we got to our bedroom, I sat on the bed and watched as Kevin undid his tie and unbuttoned his shirt. The bout we'd had in the car was fading to black as I zeroed in on his sexiness. I focused on all of the physical qualities that had made me fall for him. Kevin stood at six foot two and had the smoothest caramel-colored skin I'd ever seen in my life. Back in college he barely had a mustache, and now that he was a full-grown man, the thick 'stache connected to an even thicker beard. I didn't mind that he dyed them to keep the grays away. Hell, my hair was full of dye too. It was true that black didn't crack, but aging always had a tell somewhere. But one place it wasn't at was his body. Kevin stayed in the gym faithfully putting in work, and the six-pack that showed without him having to flex was proof of that. As I watched him undress, I bit my finger.

"Kevin?"

"Hmm?" he asked and looked over his shoulder at me.

"Come here," I told him and spread my legs, giving him a view of my lace thong.

The sight of my pussy used to make him quiver in anxiousness. All he wanted to do was fuck me. Hell, if the man could have lived in it, he would have. But apparently more than him not paying bills had changed. He shook his head at me.

"Babe, I'm stuffed. All I want to do is take a shower and then a nap right after. You know I have a long workweek ahead of me."

"I can't even get any head?" I asked, hating that I sounded as if I was begging him.

It was ridiculous because I *was*. I was lying there with my legs spread wide open, begging my husband to fuck me. I tried to seduce him some more by moving my panties to the side and showing him how wet I was. However, he barely took a glance.

"Imani, I just said I'm tired. Why don't you use one of your vibrators while I'm in the shower?"

"I know you didn't just tell me to use a sex toy when there's some dick right in front of me!" I was astonished to say the least. I closed my legs and stood up. "We haven't had sex in a month, Kevin!"

"Here we go again," he sighed and ran a hand over his face. "Imani, we both have been busy with work!"

"The way I've been the only one taking care of business around here, I can't tell! Who is she?"

"Huh?" he asked.

The bewildered look on his face made me even more frustrated. He had the nerve to act taken aback by the question. Like any woman who hadn't been so much as touched by their husband wouldn't wonder the same thing. Everyone knew that what a man wasn't getting at home he was getting somewhere else.

"You heard me. Who the hell is she?" I asked louder. "The Kevin I know is damn near a sex addict. You used to live in this pussy, and now I can't even get you to look at it. I'm not fucking stupid! The money, the phone call in the car . . . You're cheating on me. So I want to know who she is."

"Imani, you clearly had too much to drink if you think I'd ever cheat on you. I just said I've been busy at work."

"And like I said, the broke tendencies lately aren't matching up with that story."

"You know what? I'm about to take a shower and a nap. I'm not having this conversation anymore." He snatched some clothes out of his drawer and went toward the bathroom connected to our bedroom.

"Don't walk away fro—"

"Imani, it's done." His deep voice seemed to get deeper, and he shot me a look he never gave me before.

That alone stopped me in my tracks. I let him go into the bathroom and slightly jumped when he slammed the door in my face. He'd never talked to me like that, and it scared me. Not because of his tone of voice, but because it was then that I really knew he was hiding something.

These roses are almost as beautiful as you. . . .

Chapter 2

Logan

"Miss Jamison, I asked for these papers on my desk an hour ago!"

The tyrannosaurus rex shouting at me was none other than my bullheaded boss, Bethany Liner. Her icy blue eyes were piercing when I walked into her large corner office. As hard as she was staring at me, I was positive she had X-ray vision and could see my pink Vicky Secrets through my skirt suit. Bethany was a middle-aged white woman from the Bronx. She had the pinkest lips I'd ever seen, and they never smiled. That might have been for the best, however. With all of the Botox in her cheeks it would probably be a scary sight. Her hair was shoulder length and completely blond. Although she claimed it was natural, everybody knew it wasn't. At her age there should have at least been one gray on her head, but there wasn't a single strand.

I forced a smile on my face as I set the folder of processed claims down on her desk. As expected, my smile wasn't returned. Her office was as cold as her gaze. There were times where I felt that dropping out of college to pursue my dreams of being an artist wasn't the smartest thing to do. As my mother always reminded me, had I gotten my degree, I would be in Bethany's chair and not working out of a cubicle. But I didn't mind working as an insurance specialist at Lakeside.

"I'm sorry. I fell behind due to the workload being doubled last minute," I told her, forcing a chipper tone out of my mouth.

She rolled her eyes and slid the folder in front of her. After taking a moment to sift through it, she put it to the side and focused her attention back on me. "I don't need any slackers working for me, do you understand?"

"Understood," I answered quickly.

"Good. Let me ask you something, Miss Jamison. Are you happy working here?"

"I'm good at my job," I told her.

"That's not what I asked you. I asked, are you happy working here?"

I paused for a moment. It sounded like a trick question. The kind that, if I didn't answer right, could cost me my job. Knowing that Bethany's temper was short, I quickly came up with something to say.

"The work environment is pleasant, and I enjoy coming in and seeing my coworkers every day. The job itself is a piece of cake. However, who doesn't want more money? Especially with all of the new clients we're taking on and how heavy our workload has gotten." The last part kind of slipped out.

When I played it back in my head, I wanted to kick myself. No, I wanted to hurry out of the office. I was a bold woman, but at work I tried to stay in my place. Mainly because outside of that job, all I had was my artwork, and that didn't bring a steady check in every month. I cleared my throat and prepared to apologize for my forwardness, but she held a hand up to stop me from speaking.

"We're taking on another health provider, Whitman's Hospital. This is a big contract, and I don't need anything to fudge this up," Bethany said and then sighed. "I understand with all of the new clients, there's more work to be done, and that work falls on all of you."

"Yes, it does," I said, unsure of where the conversation was going.

"I want the morale on the floor to be where it needs to be to keep this ship afloat," she continued. "And that's why I wanted to know if you were happy. And now I know you're not."

"I never said—"

Bethany put another hand up to silence me. "So I've made the decision to give everyone a raise and a bonus. And you, Miss Jamison? I'm looking to give you a promotion and your own office."

"Oh, Bethany. I would love that!"

"I'm sure you would. However, it all depends on your performance when the reps from Whitman's Hospital come to view our office at the end of the week. They are our newest client, but also our biggest. I need you and everybody else to put your game faces on. Can you do that for me?"

"Yes, of course I can. Especially if I get Patricia's old office with the city view," I said, sighing in bliss, thinking about the beautiful office.

"Don't bring up that wretched woman's name ever again in my presence!" Bethany scowled, and my eyes got wide.

"Okay. I won't ever speak of her again," I said. I tapped my fingers together, and then not able to help myself, I asked, "What did she do?"

"She's the reason why our contract with Flagstaff fell through. She was sleeping with Tom Hick!"

"Wait, isn't he the VP of Texicam?" I asked.

Texicam was Lakeside's biggest competition. The two companies fought neck and neck to close the biggest contracts with new and existing healthcare providers. I had no idea that Patricia was sleeping with Tom. That was bad for business all around, especially since she'd been Bethany's right hand. She knew everything Bethany knew.

"Yes, that's him. He was able to close the deal with Flagstaf under our nose because of information Patricia fed him. But guess what?" Bethany smiled. "The joke was on her. After he got what he wanted, he dropped her like a hot potato, and I fired her. No man or job. That's a double whammy."

"Wow," I said, shaking my head. "So her job is the one I'll be filling?"

"Prove yourself to me, and we'll see. Now get out of my office so I can enjoy my lasagna."

I turned around in my three-inch Louboutin pumps and got out of there before she could change her mind about giving me a shot at a promotion. When I returned to my cubicle, I smiled when I noticed a small bouquet of flowers on my desk that wasn't there when I left. I sat down and admired the roses before reading the note that came with them. Well, I tried to read it anyway. One minute the little white paper was in my hand, and the next it was being snatched from me.

"Hey!" I exclaimed and turned to face the culprit.

The person standing behind my desk chair was Kimberly, my colleague and friend. She sat in the cubicle next to mine, and we often passed the time talking and laughing together. Like me, Kimberly was a beautiful and fiery black chick who came from a well-to-do family. Except, unlike me, she was born and raised in New York. She wore her short hair in finger waves and always wore red lip-stick. That day was no exception.

"Okay, Daddy Nathan! Sending you roses with this sweet note: 'These roses are almost as beautiful as you.' Awwww, girl! He is so nice!"

"Give me that!" I snatched the note away from her and read the words for myself.

Nate was a guy I was currently dating. It had only been a few months, so it was still relatively new. I liked him a lot, and the butterflies I felt in my stomach right then spoke for themselves. He was the perfect gentleman, and me packing a few extra pounds never seemed to bother him. He seemed to prefer a voluptuous woman, but a part of me was still waiting for the ball to drop. I couldn't remember the last time I made it out of the honeymoon stage, and that wasn't the only thing.

"Is he still cumming super early when you have sex?" Kimberly asked, taking her seat.

"Kimberly!" I exclaimed and looked around to make sure nobody had heard her.

"What? I'm just asking a question."

"Loud as hell, might I add. Damn, girl! Gon' have all these folks in here knowing I got that crack pussy between my legs!" We shared a laugh. "But on a serious note, yes, he is! He says it's because he's so attracted to me, which I get because I'm fine as hell. But I need some *stamina*."

"I know that's right. Have you tried any exercises with him to get him to last longer?"

"See that's the thing. I haven't exactly told him that I'm unsatisfied in the bedroom."

"Logan!"

"I know, I know. He's just so sweet!" I pouted. "I just don't want to bruise his ego. Plus, he should know that I'm not satisfied, right? I mean, it should be obvious."

"It should be, but I guarantee you it's not. If you don't speak up about what you want, a man won't have any problem with using you as a human masturbation device," Kimberly said, pursing her lips at me.

"So what should I do?"

"Talk to him about it. You're sitting up here worried about bruising his ego when *he* should be focused on bruising that cat."

"Hello!" I agreed, and we slapped hands. I sighed and pushed the roses to the side. "I'll talk to him. Because I def need to get my rocks off before my girls' trip."

"Oh, yeah! With your best friends from college, right? Where are you guys going this time?"

"Bali."

"I thought you guys already went there."

"We did two summers ago, but Dez *loved* it there, and it's her turn to choose, so that's where we're going. I'm sure we'll have a ball like we did the first time. Oh," I said, suddenly remembering what Bethany had told me. "We have clients coming Friday. The T-Rex wants us to act like we love our jobs, and I'm sure she'll want Friday's workload on Thursday, so you know what that means."

"Pull some magic tricks out of our ass," Kimberly groaned.

"Exactly."

He had a hardworking, sexy wife, and all he could do was complain. . . .

Chapter 3

Roze

If there was one thing I hated in the world, it was traffic. Which was something Atlanta was famous for, and there I was stuck in it. I didn't know why I thought blaring on my horn would make things go any faster, because it sure didn't. All I got back was dirty looks and the middle finger.

"Come on. Come on!" I said and hit the steering wheel.

Things were moving slower that day because of some construction on the interstate. I kept looking at the clock on the dash and getting more upset by the minute. As a prestigious real estate agent in my city, I often worked long hours to sell homes and other properties. That day had been no different, except for the fact that I completely forgot our nanny was on vacation. It had been my responsibility to go pick my girls up from school, and I completely blanked. I was already thirty minutes late when the school was blowing up my phone, and that time had bumped up to an hour. Isaiah was not going to be happy with me in the least bit. Isaiah was my husband of nine years, and let's just say things could be better between us. Much better. He already felt that I was too wrapped up in my career, so if he found out I forgot to pick up our daughters, there would be hell to pay.

Finally, traffic started to move, and I was able to make it to my exit. I drove like a madwoman the rest of the way to the school. When I finally got there, I saw my girls sitting outside with a teacher standing behind them. I could tell by the teacher's face that she was beyond annoyed. However, that expression changed to a relieved one when I came rushing up the walkway toward my daughters. Aaliyah, my oldest at 10, jumped up when she saw me approach.

"Mama, Mrs. Scatt was talking so much stuff about you before you pulled up!" she said, grabbing her bag.

"Aaliyah!" Mrs. Scatt exclaimed, wide-eyed.

"That's our mom! You thought we weren't going to tell her that you called her unfit?" My 8-year-old Maya jumped up with her hand on her hip.

Mrs. Scatt stood there looking flustered like any woman called out for her mess. I was a firm believer in standing on anything you said, but right then I just wanted to get my girls and go home.

That old white woman could think whatever she wanted about me as long as my girls were good.

"Come on, get in the car," I told them after they both gave me a hug. They raced to the car and left me standing there with Mrs. Scatt. I offered her an apologetic look. "I'm so sorry I'm late. I completely forgot that our nanny is on vacation."

"So you're telling me you forgot about your children? The very same ones you carried in your womb?" Mrs. Scatt looked distastefully at me over her spectacles.

"I got caught up at work. I was in the middle of closing a million-dollar property. It won't happen again."

"Hm."

Mrs. Scatt rolled her eyes slightly and turned away from me. I wanted to grab a fistful of her thinning hair, but I didn't need an assault charge filed against me. So instead of doing anything crazy, I just walked back to my Audi A8 and drove the girls home.

"Mommy, why were you late to get us?" Maya asked from the back seat.

"I was just wrapped up in work and forgot Nina would be gone for the week. I'm sorry, sweet girl. Do you forgive me?"

"If you buy me that new Glitter Girl backpack we saw at the mall," Maya said sneakily.

"And I want the new Jordans that came out," Aaliyah added. "I don't want to *accidentally* tell Dad that you forgot us."

"Are you two blackmailing me?" I asked, genuinely taken aback.

"I don't even know what blackmailing is," Aaliyah said, but I caught her winking at Maya in the rearview mirror.

"It's exactly what you're doing to me right now. We don't blackmail in this family, young lady," I said sternly but eventually ended up smirking despite myself. They reminded me so much of myself at their age it drove me crazy. I sighed. "Send pictures of what you want to my phone, but this stays between us, understand?"

"Roger that, Captain. What's for dinner?"

"Maya, I swear all you care about is eating! You better slow down before you get those wide hips like Grandma!"

"Stop it, Aaliyah! I don't want a big butt like Grandma!" Maya shouted back.

I listened to them bicker back and forth for what felt like forever. The only thing that seemed to end it was when we stopped and grabbed ice cream on the way. The girls thought it was another apologetic gesture for being late, which it was. But it also gave me an alibi for why I was getting home later than usual. When we arrived home, Isaiah's car was parked in its usual spot in our driveway.

I hit the opener for our three-car garage, and the girls jumped out and ran inside our family's two-story, five-bedroom home. I sighed before getting out myself.

A cloud was what I should have been on. I mean, yes, I was late getting the girls, but I'd also done a million-dollar deal earlier. Not only that, but it was my second in the last two weeks. My hard work was paying off, but for some reason it didn't seem like it. It just felt like the past year my wins didn't mean anything to Isaiah. In fact, the more I won, the more he knew I'd never give up being a working woman. My husband wanted so badly for me to be a stay-at-home wife and mother, which were things I never aspired to solely be. He didn't seem to understand that outside of those things I was an individual, too.

Finally, I got out of my car and walked in the summer heat to the garage. I couldn't wait to relax and catch up on a few of my shows. When I got in the house, I closed the garage door and entered the hallway that led to the kitchen. A groan instantly came from my mouth when I smelled the aroma from the oven. It didn't stink, but it reminded me that Isaiah had asked me to cook dinner that evening. I still could have. It was still early. But if it wasn't done his way and in his time, Isaiah would always take initiative to do it himself.

"Hey, baby," I said, stepping into the kitchen.

Isaiah was standing in front of the oven and taking a piece of foil off of his glass dish. He'd made his famous Tater Tots casserole for dinner, a favorite with the girls. I took my husband's image in, and I had to admit, he was looking mighty handsome. He was full black but had light skin and soft hair that he kept cut short. He had always been a pretty boy, which was why I almost didn't give him the time of day. In my younger years, I liked my men a little rough around the edges. And there was Isaiah, a clean-dressing, smooth-talking schoolboy. Obviously, he changed my mind. I fell in love with him, and we got married. I thought we would have a forever happily ever after, but things between us were fragile lately. When he turned and faced me, he didn't return the smile I was giving him. In fact, he had a look of downright disappointment.

"You forgot them?" he asked incredulously.

"They said they weren't going to say anything," I growled and looked around him to see if I could spot those little traitors.

"*They* didn't tell me anything. The school called me. What the hell were you thinking?"

"Whoa, why are you cursing at me? I just got tied up closing a house at work."

"Picking your kids up from school should always be more important than any paperwork," he said, and I held my hand up.

"Isaiah, I'm not doing this right now. I got the girls, and they're safe. We're home now. That's all that matters. You're the one who wanted to put them in a year-round school, not me." I tried to walk away, but he just wasn't letting up.

"This isn't the first time you've put your job first. You missed two of Maya's volleyball games."

"And I made it to six!" I exclaimed, whipping back around to face him. "I'm not perfect. I'm human, Isaiah. What do you want me to do, give up my career?"

"Do you really want me to answer that?"

"You're so selfish!"

"Is it really selfish to want my wife at home raising our children? Most women would be happy to have a man willing to provide for them. With the money I make at the firm, we would be more than okay without your income."

"You knew when you married me that I was an ambitious woman." I pointed my finger at him.

"And I guess I thought it would change once we had children. You know what? This conversation isn't getting us anywhere. I'm done."

I scoffed as I watched him begin to prepare the dinner table. I noticed that he only got three plates from the cabinet. My hand found my hip, and my neck rolled, showcasing my attitude, because I just knew he wasn't doing what I thought he was doing.

"So you aren't going to make my plate?"

"I figured you wouldn't have any problem making it yourself since you're so independent."

I groaned loudly and stormed out of the kitchen and upstairs to our bedroom. Once there, I shut the door and balled my hands into fists in the air. I couldn't believe he was being such a jerk! My daughters meant everything to me, so him throwing in the two games I'd missed was a low blow. The only reason he was able to make it to everything was because he could choose the days he worked from home. I didn't have that luxury. Also, as a working woman, I always made it a point to be present as much as possible so my girls knew I was invested in them. But it was also important to me that they see a successful black woman handling business at home *and* in the work field. Women were so much more than wives and moms! I wanted both of them to chase their dreams no matter what. So it hurt that he would use that against me. Not only that, but he had some nerve telling me what I should be grateful for.

I paced the room to calm myself down because I hated being upset in front of Aaliyah and Maya. Eventually, my heartbeat slowed, and my breathing was back to normal. I walked to our long dresser against the wall and stared into the mirror. I took myself in and stood up straighter. The woman staring back at me was brown and beautiful. She wore the flyest suit, and her wig was laid to the gods. Isaiah was the one who should be grateful. He had a hardworking, sexy wife, and all he could do was complain. He would just have to get over it. There had to be a common ground somewhere.

I turned away from the mirror and prepared to take my suit off when my eyes fell on Isaiah's suit jacket on the bed. He knew I hated outside clothes to touch our covers, but if I complained about *that*, I was being petty. I sighed and grabbed it off the bed to hang it up, but when I did, three pieces of paper fell from the breast pocket. Curious, I picked them up and saw that they were receipts. One was for a hotel in Buckhead, another was for room service for two, and the last was for an expensive bouquet of flowers. I smiled, thinking that my husband was planning to surprise me with a romantic getaway, but that smile faded when I saw the dates on the receipts. They were from the week prior. And Isaiah and I hadn't gone anywhere that week, but he *had* been gone Friday into Saturday. I hadn't thought anything of it because he was often called away to nearby cities to meet clients. It wasn't the first time he was too tired to make the drive home, but it was the first time I'd ever known him to share a room with anybody. Especially not somebody he was buying flowers for.

My heart dropped. I knew things between us were rocky, but I never thought they would get that far. Mama didn't raise a fool. Isaiah was cheating on me.

What's done in the dark always gets brought to the light. . . .

Chapter 4

Desiree

It was only six o'clock in Atlanta, and I found myself snuggled in bed under my covers, watching reruns of *Martin*. I'd seen them so many times that I could recite them word for word. Sheneneh was my favorite with her crazy self. However, that evening it seemed as if the show were watching me more than I was watching it. I was so tired, and my body ached. I was trying to stay awake because I was expecting an important call that hadn't come yet.

I sighed and leaned back on my pillows. Most would say a grown woman in her mid-thirties who just lay in bed had to have been depressed. But my bedroom was my happy place. I'd filled it with all of the things I loved. One of them was pictures. Every wall was covered in pictures that held my fondest memories. Among them were a plethora of photos of me and my very best friends. Roze,

Logan, and Imani were more like sisters to me. We were beautiful black women of all shades, me being the most chocolate out of the bunch. In college, we all but had the boys on campus eating crumbs out of our hands.

Roze and I had grown up together thick as thieves since our mothers lived in the same apartment complex. We met Logan and Imani our first year of college, and we became inseparable. Even when both Logan and Imani moved out of state to pursue their dreams, we remained close. In fact, we started our own travel club called the Travelistas. That way, we would for sure see each other for a week every year. Sometimes we were able to get away together more frequently, but that one week in the summer was law for us. It was one we always looked forward to.

We all took turns who would choose and plan the trip, and this time was my turn. Usually, we would go to new places we'd never been, but I decided to go back to Bali. I'd fallen in love with the waters and sights there. My soul yearned to go back. The only one who had an issue with it was Imani, and that was only because she wanted so badly to go to Tokyo. She would have her time to do that, but she would have to wait.

On the nightstand next to my bed, my phone rang. Hoping it was the person I was waiting for, I hurried to pick it up. Only it wasn't who I was expecting. It was Imani.

"I must have thought you up," I said when I answered.

"That's because you know there's a 911 situation going on," she said almost breathlessly into the phone.

"Girl, are you running? You sound like you can't breathe."

"That's because I had to run off to my office to call you! Dez, you aren't going to believe this, but I think Kevin is cheating again!"

"Again?" I made a face and sat up. "I don't remember the first time."

"Dez, you don't remember when I caught him having coffee with that bitch?"

"You mean his colleague?"

"Colleague, side chick. What's the difference these days?" she asked, and I couldn't help but laugh.

"I'm sorry, girl. But the only thing I remember from that was that you were never able to prove he was cheating."

"Well, it was suspicious, just like now. Do you know he's been short on bills the last few months? *And* he keeps conveniently forgetting his wallet at home whenever we go eat or do something. And I called his job. He still works there. So the money is still coming in."

"So how does this equate to him cheating?"

"He has to be spending all his money on another woman! You know these new-age bitches are expensive! Where else could his money be going?"

"Have you asked him about it?"

"Yes, but all he says is that I should trust him. And he threw in my face how he supported me when we first got to L.A."

"Which he did."

"Whose side are you on here?" she asked, and I sighed.

"Ni Ni, all I'm saying is I think you should do some more digging before you jump to those conclusions. You owe him that much. Plus, the solution could be a simple one."

"Or he could be cheating," she said as my phone began to beep in my ear.

"Let me call you back. Somebody's on my other line." I clicked over before she could object. "Hello?"

"Oh, my God, finally you answered! I don't know how someone who's off all summer for break can be so busy!" It was Logan.

"See, that's your problem. You confuse my free time with my availability."

"Whatever, you could have called me back," Logan pouted like the grown baby she was.

"Why would I do that if you were just going to call me again?" I teased.

One thing my friends were going to do was call me and tell me about the things going on in their lives, and vice versa. I oftentimes found that my phone got blown up more than the others, especially in the summertime due to public school being out. I'd been a teacher for almost a decade, and having summers off was always a treat. It gave me time to unwind and enjoy my life. It also made me a part-time and unpaid counselor to three crazy black women.

"See? I should hang up on your ass. I was calling to talk about Nate."

"Oh, the new boo. How are things going with him?"

"They're so good. He's really the nicest man I've dated in so long. He has a good job, he treats me how I want to be treated, and, girl, the man knows how to communicate! Not to mention he bought me my first pair of Louboutins that weren't hand-me-downs from Imani!"

"Okay, these are all great things, but I can't help but feel like the ball is about to drop," I presumed, and she sighed.

"Dez, you know I'm a freak, and this man has yet to rock my world! He's a minute man," she exclaimed, and I had to hold back my laughter. "He says it's because he's so attracted to me, but it's frustrating. All that meat he's packing turns into a noodle dick in three minutes. I mean, what am I supposed to do?"

"And I'm guessing you think talking to him about it will bruise his ego and make him pull away from you?"

"Yes! And I really like him, so I don't want that. But I just don't know what to do."

"Hmm. This is serious," I said and tapped my chin.

And it was, because, like she had said, Logan was a freak. She spoke the language of sex fluently and had made it clear since college that if a man lacked in the bedroom, it was a deal breaker. I knew she really liked Nate because had he been anyone else giving her that problem, she would have been out the door. Still, that move might be around the corner. Being as she was the only one of us who hadn't been married, I for one was rooting for her to have something stable.

"Maybe try having sex in pitch blackness?" I suggested. "Or maybe put a blindfold on him."

"Ooh, I never thought of that."

"You know eighty percent of a man's sexual experience is visual. So maybe him not being turned on by seeing you will help him last longer."

"Is it really eighty percent?"

"Girl, I don't know. I pulled that number out of my ass," I admitted, and we both laughed. My phone beeped in my ear again, and when I looked, I saw that it was Roze. "Oop, this is Roze. Try what I just said, and let me know how it goes. Also, get in the group chat so we can talk about last minute details about the trip."

"Okay, talk to you later. I love you."

She dropped off and I clicked over. I had a small smile on my face. Talking to them always put me in a good mood. That same smile went away in seconds when I heard what sounded like sniffling on the other end of the phone.

"Roze? Is everything okay?"

"No," she said softly. "It's Isaiah. We got into a fight."

"Oh, no. What happened?"

"I forgot the girls at school today."

"Roze."

"I know, I know. I just got so wrapped up at work, but I got them. I was just late. But Isaiah was so mad. It just fueled the fire he has of wanting me to stop working."

"I mean, I understand his frustration, but wanting you to give up your career is crazy talk. He knows how much your work means to you."

"Apparently he doesn't. He keeps talking about how he can cover our lifestyle and I need to just be a stay-at-home wife. He had the nerve to say any other woman would be grateful for that opportunity."

"Does he know what year it is? We like to work and make our own money, sir."

"Exactly, but it's deeper than that for me. I want my girls to know that they'll always be more than just a reproduction body and maid for a man. He doesn't get it."

"I'm so sorry, Roze. But I'm sure he'll come around. He loves you."

"I don't know about that anymore either," Roze said and broke into a fit of sobs. "He's cheating on me."

"I doubt that. Isaiah's not the type to step out on his family," I said, trying to reassure her, thinking she was just being dramatic like Imani.

"I know he is. I found a hotel receipt and another for room service in his jacket pocket."

"That's normal though, right? He goes out of town for business all the time."

"Room service for two! And I saw a receipt for expensive flowers. And he lied to me. He told me he was in Savannah, but the receipt said he was in Buckhead."

"Damn," was all I could think of to say, and it made her cry even harder.

"I don't know what I'm going to do, Dez. All I have is my family."

"Oh, you have so much more than that. And we don't even know for sure if he's doing anything. Just sit on it and keep your eyes peeled. What's done in the dark always gets brought to the light. And if something does come up, we'll deal with it then, together, like we always have. Okay?"

"Okay." She sniffled.

For the third time, my phone beeped in my ear. I glanced at the screen and saw that it was finally the phone call I was waiting for. I didn't want to leave Roze high and dry like that, but the call was important.

"I'm going to call you tomorrow, okay? I love you." I clicked over after she said it back, and I took a deep breath. "Hello, Dr. Palmer."

"Good evening, Desiree." Dr. Palmer's voice came through smoothly. "I'm sorry to be calling you so late, but we got the results from your most recent lab back."

"And?" I asked, holding my breath.

"I'm so sorry. It seems like that last round of chemo just didn't work as well as we thought. The cancer has spread."

Frankly, I don't give a damn what you need. . . .

Chapter 5

Dez

I didn't know if it was fear or the need for comfort that put me in front of my parents' house. Our family home was where I'd grown up. I stared at the front door for a while, not knowing why I didn't go in. Maybe it was because I was ashamed. I hadn't told my parents about my first run-in with the deadly disease, because I just knew I'd beaten it. And I had, temporarily. I knew it was possible for the cancer to come back, but I thought I'd be one of the cases where it didn't. I couldn't help but feel punished for being so foolish to think I was favored. I knew I didn't have the strength to fight alone this time. But still, I hesitated at that front door. Instead of walking through it, I looked around and took in everything nearby.

I could still feel the tickle from the grassy glade as I ran barefoot as a girl and the gusts of wind on my face as I went as high as I could on our tree swing. Everything had changed, but at the same time it hadn't. My parents had kept up with their home and their property, but there wasn't enough money in the world that could make them take down that swing. I probably couldn't count how many photos we'd taken by it. They always joked and told me that when I had a daughter, the tradition would continue.

The lump in my throat sprang up on me as I thought about the possibility of not being able to give them grandchildren. My mama and daddy were the finest people I knew, and they would make amazing grandparents. I straightened up before I lost my nerve altogether and knocked on the door. It didn't take long for it to swing open and for my daddy to be beaming down at me. My daddy, aka Curtis Vincent, was an ox of a man. He stood at six foot three and didn't look a day over 50, although he was pushing 70. Everyone knew that black didn't crack unless you were on it. He was still handsome as ever, with his smooth brown skin and radiant smile. I remember when I was growing up that Mama had to whoop a few women behind him. These were stories that she told proudly to the day.

"Suga!" he exclaimed and held out his arms.

"Hey, Daddy," I said and let him pull me into a hug. When he let me go, I smiled up at his fresh haircut. "I see you're finally letting the grays come through."

"I have no idea what you're talking about," he said and gave me a warning look that made me laugh.

For years he thought Mama and I didn't know he was dying his hair in secret. But we knew. However, the one thing my mama taught me at an early age was to never take away a man's youth. Let him grow old on his own. She gave me a lot of man advice, actually. Funny how my marriage fell apart before I barely got to use any of it.

"Is Mama home?" I asked, stepping into the house.

"Yup. Back in the kitchen. You must have known she's whipping up a pot of seafood gumbo for dinner tonight."

"I didn't, but I'm glad I picked today to come by!"

He chuckled and locked the door behind me. We walked back to the kitchen together, passing all of our family portraits on the walls. Growing up, I always felt that we had a television sitcom house. Everything was staged perfectly. But I guess that just spoke for my mother's superb decorating and coordinating skills. Her back was to us when we entered the kitchen, and I smiled watching her petite frame move around the kitchen. She was humming, something she did when she was in a good mood. It almost made me sad, knowing what I'd come to tell them. My daddy cleared his throat, and she turned her head quickly around.

"Hey, Mama," I said.

She dropped the seasonings she was holding on the marble counter and came over to me. Happy wouldn't be enough to describe the expression on her face when she saw me. The way my parents treated me whenever I came over, a person would think I visited once a year instead of a few times a week. Mama hugged me tightly, and when she let me go, she cupped my cheek in her hand. I tried not to look too long into her eyes, knowing she had the power to sense when something was off about me. However, once she fixated on me, I could see her mind start to go to work.

"Desiree, is everything all right?" she asked, dropping her hand.

"Yes, Mama, why wouldn't it be?"

"Well, you usually let somebody know when you're stopping by. Shoot, I would have had dinner ready by now if I'd expected you."

"Woman, leave the girl alone," my daddy said, butting in. "She just got here. She doesn't need to be interrogated."

"Thanks, Daddy," I said, giving him a grateful look before turning back to her. "And, Mama, there is something I want to talk to you guys about, but it can wait until after dinner."

"Mm-hmm. Well, whatever you have to tell us, I hope it doesn't have anything to do with that devil Caleb," Mama said, going back to her seasonings and her gumbo pot.

At the mention of my ex-husband's name, my mother got a sour look on her face. I wasn't fond of him, but Mama didn't like him at all, especially after our divorce. I hadn't seen or talked to him in some time, and I'd recently taken him off of my insurance. For all I knew he was out somewhere living his best life.

"Why do you say that?" I asked.

"He's been poking around here looking for you," my father said, sitting down at the kitchen table. "Keeps trying to get us to tell him your new address and phone number."

"You haven't given it to him, have you?"

"Of course not!" Mama chimed in.

I was relieved. Caleb wasn't a danger to me or anything like that, but I was the kind of person who, when I moved on, I moved *on*. Entirely. There was nothing in that past for me, and the one thing Caleb decided he didn't want to do was treat me right. So in the past was where he would stay. He hadn't bothered me in almost a year, or so I thought. Hearing that he'd been looking for me was a strange revelation, and I couldn't figure out what it was he could possibly want.

"Did he say what he wanted?"

"No. Just that he wanted us to tell you to call him. I thought if I didn't tell you, then you'd never call and he would leave you alone," Mama said.

"Well, when's the last time he was here?"

"Yesterd—"

Ding-dong!

The doorbell ringing interrupted Mama, and Daddy went to go see who it was. Mama went back to cooking, and I leaned against the pantry door with a million thoughts running through my mind. A big part of me knew what Caleb wanted, but he

would get it over my dead body. A few moments
later, Daddy returned to the kitchen, but he had
somebody with him. It was Caleb. I almost spit my
juice out, except I wasn't drinking any. When he
saw me, he had a slight smirk on his caramel face.

"Speak of the devil," Mama said with a glare.

"I feel special. Y'all were just talking about little
old me?" Caleb asked and feigned surprise.

"Just about how you won't take the hint and go
on somewhere."

"Debra, no need to be rude," Daddy said, shooting her a look. She puffed and turned back to
the food. "Caleb would like to have a word with
Desiree. But, suga, if you don't want to talk, I'll
send this joker packing. But unlike your mama, I
won't make the choice for you."

I bit down on my teeth as I stared at my ex-husband. He hadn't changed a bit since the last time
I saw him. In fact, he might have been wearing
the same suit. Caleb was a hotshot lawyer who
seemed to always have a smug look on his face.
Especially when he got what he wanted. And right
then, a conversation with me was clearly what he
wanted. I wanted to deny him of that right and win
the small victory, but I figured one conversation
wouldn't hurt. I nodded my head at Daddy, letting
him know it was okay. I waved for Caleb to follow
me. I almost went to the sitting room, but knowing my parents, they would be listening in on our
conversation. So instead, I took him upstairs to my
old bedroom. I stepped inside and let the cool air

hit my face. I could tell Mama had been inside recently, because the plug-in on the wall had been changed, and the sweet aroma of vanilla coursed through the room. Not to mention there wasn't a dust speck in sight. I turned on a lamp and sat on my tall queen-sized bed, motioning for him to sit at the wooden desk by the tall window.

"So what's this I hear about you wanting to talk to me?" I asked, crossing my arms.

As a lawyer, it was Caleb's job to read body language, so I kept mine under control. While we were married, Caleb had been very controlling. Unluckily for him, I'd been raised by two strong black people, and it was damn near impossible to put me in check. I could never be the weak wife he wanted, and that was just one of the things that led to our divorce.

"You know exactly why I'm here, Dez," he said evenly.

"I'm sorry if you think I can read minds, Caleb. But I can't. Like I tell my students, please use your words."

His palm slammed down on the top of the desk, but I didn't jump. In fact, I didn't even blink. It didn't take long for his put-together exterior to piece away.

"Dammit, Dez. Don't play these games with me. Where is my money?"

"What money?"

"Dez, I swear to God—"

"*Ohhh!* You mean the money you stole from your clients and hid in the walls of the house that was in *my* name?"

"Yes, that money."

"I don't know where that is," I said with a shrug.

Did I mention that my ex-husband was a crook? I found out when I accidently put a huge hole in the wall of our home. I tried to patch it up myself, but when I reached in the hole to grab what had fallen through, I pulled out a lot more than just drywall. Try a stack of money wrapped in plastic. That was the day I knew I'd had enough. And after some snooping through his laptop, I found that he was robbing his clients blind.

"Dez, stop playing with me. That was half a million dollars. Where is it? I need it. Now!"

"Frankly, I don't give a damn what you need, Caleb. Did you forget how you treated me when we were married? All those late nights away. All the women?" I scoffed. "And then you have the nerve to hide money in the walls of the house my parents gifted me after our wedding."

"All that is irrelevant to me now. I just want my money, and you have until the end of today to get it to me."

His words mixed with the intense look in his eyes made me laugh.

"You have some nerve. Caleb, you aren't in the position to give me an ultimatum. Need I remind you of how you got that money in the first place?"

"It's money I saved from cases I worked," he said through clenched teeth.

"More like money you stole," I chuckled. "I went through your files back then, Caleb. I know what you did."

"You don't know shit!"

"I know that as the lawyer to many high-end clients, you had access to their bank accounts. Millionaires, a few billionaires. People who wouldn't even notice money missing from their accounts. And you did it so many times over the years. A crook is what you are."

"Dez, you're gonna give me that money. Or you're gonna wish you had!" Caleb jumped to his feet and came at me with his hands outstretched.

I was quicker than him though. When I was 15, my father gave me a .22. He told me to put it in a place where I'd be able to get to it if ever he weren't there to protect me. I grabbed it from under my pillow and pointed it at Caleb's face, stopping him in his tracks.

"Ooh. I bet you were angry when I finally let you get your things from the house and you found the walls empty," I laughed. "You'll never see that money. And if you keep harassing me, I'll turn you in. You thought I didn't make copies of everything I found in your laptop? Why do you think I didn't fight for alimony in the divorce? Now get the hell out. And if you come by my parents' house again,

I'll hire someone to wipe you off the face of the earth. We both know I can afford it."

If looks could kill, I would have been a dead woman right then and there. But Caleb backed off and didn't do anything stupid, which I was glad about. I talked a good game, but I could never kill someone. Or hire someone to kill. However, he didn't know that.

The saddest part about the whole exchange was that there was a point in time where Caleb and I really loved each other. I couldn't even pinpoint when it began to fizzle out. It just happened one day. He just changed. He'd turned into someone I didn't recognize, and that was the person standing on the other end of my gun. He jerked on his suit jacket before pointing at me.

"You're going to regret this," he said and left the room.

The way he said it made my body turn cold, like I was sitting in a bucket of ice. Suddenly, I lost all the nerve to tell my parents the truth about why I'd come over. I didn't want to think about it at all.

Are you done? . . .

Chapter 6

Logan

I bustled around my apartment at midnight to make sure I hadn't forgotten anything while packing. I left for Bali in the morning, and I wanted to be fully prepared for a week with my favorite girls. So far my biggest suitcase was completely full, and I was debating taking another suitcase or just a duffle for my miscellaneous items.

"Babe, come lie down with me."

The deep baritone voice sent chills down my spine. It came from behind me on my bed. I smirked slyly as I turned to face the sexy hunk of a man lying there in nothing but a durag and his briefs. Nate's muscular golden skin glistened under the light of the room, and he flashed his pearly whites at me. He had the room smelling lovely since he'd just gotten out of the shower, but the way he was looking at me let me know he was ready to get dirty again.

"Baby, I can't. I'm packing."

"You look packed to me," he told me.

"I just don't want to forget anything. Last time I forgot my whole bag of underwear and it was so bad!"

"Ain't nothing wrong with free balling here and there."

"Boy, you see all this ass and you know how fat this cat is. I cannot free ball!"

"You're right. Plus, I don't want anybody getting a peek at my goodies." Nate got up from the bed and came behind me. When he wrapped his arms around my waist, I felt his hard manhood press against my butt. "I love how thick you are. It turns me on so much."

The feel of his warm breath on my ear right before he nibbled it got the faucet leaking. A moan escaped my mouth, and that was all the confirmation he needed to continue. He turned me to face him, and our lips met in a passionate, wet kiss. He undressed me as our tongues danced, only breaking our kiss to step back and gaze at my body. I was a thicker woman, but I had a shape, and my stomach was flat. Still, I was over 200 pounds and only average height, which meant I was overweight. I used to be self-conscious about my body, but eventually it got to a point where I began to love myself and my curves. Nate did too, and he had no trouble showing it.

As he stared at me, he pulled his thick eight-inch sausage out of his boxers and stroked it slowly while staring at me. I grinned devilishly and pushed him back on the bed. Completely naked, I dropped down on all fours and crawled to him, never breaking eye contact. When I reached the bed, I pulled his boxers completely off and licked him from balls to tip.

"Hsss!" he hissed as I wrapped my lips completely around the tip of his dick.

I moved my entire mouth down his shaft until he hit the back of my throat, and even then I kept going. Deep throating was my specialty, and I loved doing it to him. Soon the only sound that could be heard in the air was me sucking and slurping and not leaving any crumbs. I wanted to add the two-hand-twist combo, but I knew that was going to make him climax way too early, and I wanted to feel him inside of me. My vaginal walls contracted and retracted, letting me know I was getting hornier by the second. His moans and the way he was gripping the back of my head were turning me on. I came up for air and wiped all of the spit from my mouth.

"Fuck me," I said, but when he tried to pull me onto the bed, I held up a finger. "Hold on."

I decided to take Dez's advice. When I stood up, I walked to the light switch and turned the lights off. I also went to the window and shut the curtains so that it was pitch-black.

"What are you doing?" he asked as he was putting a condom on.

"I thought we'd try something new tonight," I said.

I felt my way back to the bed and straddled him. I wanted to ride him, but he had other plans. Nate flipped me on my back and kissed all over my body. When he got to my nipples, I sucked air through my teeth. I loved when he licked and sucked them. They were my second-most tender spot. While he did that, he circled a finger on my clit, bringing me to a place of bliss. I could feel my juices running down my crack and onto the bed beneath me. I could have let him make me cum like that, but I needed to feel his erection against my walls. I wanted him so bad, and he didn't make me wait much longer.

He kissed me deeply again when he got on top of me and didn't stop even when he plunged his manhood deep inside of me. And he did it again and again. I saw fireworks, and I wrapped my arms tightly around his back. His strokes were both powerful and gentle. He handled me with care.

"Nate!" I moaned. "This big dick feels so good. Fuck me!"

"Yeah, you like this big-ass dick, don't you?"

"Yes, baby."

"You ain't never had nobody fuck you like this, huh?"

I didn't answer. I just moaned. I didn't want to ruin the moment we were having. The only person who had ever done it like that was him. And I was pleasantly surprised that it was looking like he had some stamina. My clit began to swell with each thrust, and the closer I got to my orgasm, the more I felt Dez had been right. Maybe that had been the trick to his quick-pumper problem. Maybe—

"Ah . . . ahhhh!" Nate moaned and jerked a few times on top of me.

I didn't need two guesses to know what that meant. He rolled back onto the bed, breathing heavily, while I lay there in disbelief. I had literally just started to get into my groove, and then it was over. He lay there panting like he had just put it down on me, and I was flabbergasted.

"Are you done?" I blurted out.

"Yeah, baby. I'm tired, and you know I have that meeting after I take you to the airport."

"But . . . but . . ." I was at a complete loss for words.

"Plus, you have to finish packing, right?"

He had the nerve to turn over on his side and get under the covers. Like I wasn't right there unsatisfied and upset. It took everything in me to not hit him with a pillow. Most people considered being "hangry" a mixture of being hungry and angry. But in my case it meant horny and angry. Instead of hurting him, I climbed out of bed and went to take a shower. I needed to wash the disappointment off my body.

I found peace there. . . .

Chapter 7

Imani

On the morning of takeoff for the Travelistas' annual girls' trip, Kevin was given the responsibility of getting me to the airport on time. I woke up hours before him, wanting to make sure I had everything I needed. I went through my checklist and suitcases three more times before I was convinced that everything was there. The main thing I wanted to be sure about were my vibrator and dildo. There was nothing like beating your pussy up after a long day of fun in the sun. Orgasms cured everything— at least, that was my philosophy.

Anyway, checking my bags wasn't the only reason I wanted to get up early. I just couldn't shake the thought that Kevin was doing something he had no business doing, but I needed proof to accuse him of anything. After I left my store earlier in the week, I'd stopped and grabbed some nanny cams. Things had gotten so sophisticated with the times. You could get cameras that looked like regular plants or candles. I'd opted for the photo frames. That way I could put them in multiple rooms without seeming suspicious.

While Kevin was sleeping, I hung one up in our room. And once I was done packing, I put one in the living room and by the front door so I could see who came and who went. I wasn't playing with that man or my marriage. I loved my husband dearly, but I'd be damned if I just let him pull the wool over my eyes. I wasn't one of those women who would ever just let my man cheat in peace because he was a good man. Please. If I caught him doing anything while I was on vacation, he would catch the hottest part of hell. I had just hung the last photo and was completing the camera setup on my phone when I felt a strong pair of arms wrap around me. I jumped and turned around only to see my husband standing behind me.

"What was wrong with the old frame?" he asked, yawning and rubbing one of his eyes.

"Oh, nothing. I just thought these would go better with our house," I said, hurrying to put my phone in the pocket of my robe.

"Whatever you say." He shrugged. "You finish packing?"

"Yup. I'm just about to hit the shower and throw on my airport outfit."

"You women and your outfits."

"Don't start," I warned with a smile.

"I won't, but I'll tell you what I want to do," he said, looking at me in my nightgown and robe, licking his lips.

"And what's that?"

"Give you a real reason to need a shower!"

He scooped me up into his strong arms, something he hadn't done in a while, and carried me back upstairs to our bedroom. He placed me gently on the bed and removed his shirt. My eyes might have been deceiving me, but I swore it looked like my husband had been hitting the gym. I mean, the man always had a nice body, but he looked more cut that morning. Maybe it was because the light from the lamp in our room was dim. Either way he looked damn good.

"Baby, you're gonna make me late to the airport," I said.

"I'll get you there on time, I promise," he said, climbing on top of me. "I gotta send you off with a parting gift, don't I? Gotta make you remember what you have at home when you see all those shirtless island men."

He laughed at his own joke, but I didn't. He began kissing my neck and roaming my body with his hands. My eyes were on the ceiling, and although his touch felt good, my thoughts were overpowering.

"Kevin, would you ever cheat on me?"

My question clearly caught him off guard because he stopped all that he was doing abruptly. He looked at me, and I stared deeply into his brown eyes, trying to find the deception, the lies. He furrowed his brow at me and shook his head.

"I wouldn't do anything to hurt you, Imani. I love you."

Those were his words, but I just didn't believe them. But in that moment, I didn't press the issue. I could feel his hardness against my clit, and I couldn't deny that I was horny as hell. Instead of challenging his answer, I just kissed him. His tongue slid into my mouth, and we gave each other the sloppiest kiss ever. He slipped my lace panties off, and I spread my legs wide for him. One of his hands found its way to my plump pussy, and he moaned in my ear when he felt how wet I was already. He let out a shaky breath as he pulled his briefs down just enough to release his long, thick monster. The moment I felt him tap it against my clit, I remembered the reason why I would go crazy if he stepped out on me. If a woman ever got a taste of what he was working with, she wasn't going to leave him alone. Just like I hadn't been able to.

"Put it in," I begged in a whisper.

I didn't need to ask again. In a swift motion, he pierced the heart of my love tunnel with his sword and stabbed me deeply. One thing about me was that I *loved* to make love, but sometimes I just needed the shit fucked out of me. And this was one of those times. After a few slow strokes, Kevin began to pound relentlessly in and out of my poor cat. I cried out happily and bit down on his dick with my vaginal walls, trying to match his thrusts.

As he was fucking me, he stripped the rest of my clothes off. One of his hands held on to my left jiggly breast, while his other hand held my right one in place so he could suck my nipple. My pleasure senses were off the meter. Especially when his thumb began to caress the nipple that wasn't getting attention. He knew they were my spot, and just that fast, I felt my orgasm coming.

"Kevin! Kevin!"

"Let it go, baby. Let it go," he coached me.

And let it go I did. My back arched as I released my waters all over him. I could literally feel my body grow exhausted with such a powerful orgasm, but Kevin wasn't going to let me go that easily. It was his turn. He flipped me over and put me on all fours before sliding his dick back inside of me. Grabbing a handful of my freshly done hair, he forced my back to arch deeper than it ever had before. As he pounded me out, my moans barely made it out of my mouth. I couldn't even catch my breath. That man was making up for all of the nights he didn't fuck this pussy, and I was loving every second of it. With my own hand, I rubbed

my clit, because there was no way I wasn't going to
cum all over that dick again.

"Shit!" he shouted.

I knew what that meant. He was almost there. I
rubbed my clit harder and faster, wanting desper-
ately to meet him at the finish line. Finally, I felt it
swell, and my body jerked as my second orgasm
grew nearer and near—

"Ahhh!" we shouted in climax.

His was so strong that I could literally feel his
dick unloading inside of me. His hands gripped
my waist with the might of two men. When I
looked back at him, his eyes were clenched shut
and he was biting his lip. I clenched my vaginal
walls tightly, wanting to catch every drop, and he
moaned again.

"Damn, Mani. That pussy is so good. Fuck."

He caught his breath and removed himself from
inside of me. I wanted badly to roll over and go to
sleep, but a quick glance at the digital clock beside
our bed made me think better of it. I jumped up
and rushed to the shower on wobbly legs. There
wasn't a dick in the world that could make me miss
my flight or make me pay double to rebook.

"Kevin, why are you driving so slow? That geriat-
ric couple just passed us!"

"Relax, Imani, we're going to make it on time,"
he said calmly.

"Not if you keep driving like a paw-paw!" I groaned.

"That pussy has me in a daze. But let's not forget you had to catch that last part of *Grey's Anatomy* before we left the house."

"What is this? A lecture?"

"Nah, this is Paw-paw getting on your neck!"

I had to chuckle. He always knew how to make me laugh. But still that moment of lightheartedness didn't take away from the fact that I didn't trust him. Neither did the good sex he'd put on me.

I hated that I had to stoop to such measures like putting cameras in our house to try to catch him in a lie. There had been a time where I could say without batting an eye that my man was loyal to me and that he would never be unfaithful. But after you've been married so long, you start to wonder if your partner's attention is fading. Take me for example. I would never cheat on my husband, but recently I had been daydreaming about sex with other men. I figured it was because I was lacking physical touch from my counterpart. It bothered me, but it seemed that us not having sex didn't bother Kevin one bit. Our morning of passion could last him weeks, maybe months. And that led me to think that he was getting it from somewhere else.

He tried to make small talk the rest of the way to the airport, and I tried to talk back. But the truth was I wasn't really paying him any mind. I was just ready to get the long plane ride over with so I could have a fun week.

We arrived at the airport terminal an hour before takeoff, which was still cutting it short since LAX was always so busy. Kevin got out and helped me with my bags before giving me a hug and a kiss.

"You sure you don't want me to help you check your bags?"

"No, it's okay. I should be able to manage."

"All right, if you say so. Have fun and be safe, beautiful," he said. "I'll miss you."

"Will you really?" I heard myself ask.

"Huh?"

"Nothing. I love you too. Be good."

I waved and rolled my designer luggage inside of the airport to check it. That process alone took ten minutes. But once the weight was off of me, I was able to rush through TSA and toward the gate we would be flying out of. We always flew to our destination together, and that time we chose to fly out of LAX. I spotted my girls sitting together and maneuvered through the crowd in their direction.

"Sista sissstas!" I exclaimed when I reached them.

"There she is!" Dez said, getting up to hug me.

"Now how the hell is it that you live here but you're the only one who's late?" Roze asked, pulling me into an embrace.

"Girl, you know she's a last-minute everything doer. She's been like that since college. I don't know how she runs a successful business!" Dez teased.

"That's because I don't play about my money," I said, snapping my finger. "You three were over here talking shit about me, weren't you?"

"We were just saying we hope you don't miss your flight like you did when we went to Hawaii! But you got here just in time, because they're about to start boarding us," Logan said, reminding me about what a headache getting to Hawaii had been for me. "I'm just ready to get this flight over with! I need a beach in my life. Work has been kicking my ass."

"Oh, no. How's the art pursuit going? Have you sold any paintings?" I asked, sitting next to her.

Out of all of us, Logan was the one who hadn't exactly hit the ground running, for lack of a better phrase. I knew it couldn't be easy for her all alone in New York, which was why I helped her whenever I could. All of us did, really. In fact, the three of us always paid for Logan's travel expenses whenever we went anywhere. All she had to do was get the time off at work and bring spending money, which we barely let her spend. We helped her out of our love for her, but we never wanted her to feel like a charity case.

"I sold two paintings last month, which helped a lot to cover my expenses for a while. It's just hard sometimes with a full-time job," she told me.

"Girl, how many times have we told you to just take the leap of faith!" I said. "You know we got you through any ups and downs until you get things rocking and rolling."

"The three of you do too much for me already," Logan said, shaking her head. "I love the way you love me, but when I do take that leap of faith, I want to be able to hold my own weight. No pun intended."

"Not funny." Dez pointed a warning finger at her. "Girl, you look good. The thick look has always worked for you. I wish I had that much ass."

"Dez, you have a big ass!"

"Well, I want more!" She laughed.

"Girl, bye." Roze swatted the air with her hand. "Anyway, remind me why you chose to go to Bali again?"

Dez paused for a moment, and we all stared at her. There was a look of happiness that appeared in her eyes. They smiled when her lips didn't. "I found peace there. It's one of the most beautiful places I've ever been. I just wanted to see it one more time."

"It was nice the last time we went. I enjoyed it," I added.

"Not to mention those men were fine as hell! Do you remember the pool boy?" Logan inserted and put a hand to her chest. "If it weren't for the fact that I could see his shrimp dick through his trunks, I would have given his young ass a try. I know he would have gone for it, too. All this chocolate ass."

We all joined her in laughter because we knew she was serious. The thing I could say about my girls was that we were all fine as wine and had aged well. Mid-thirties wasn't old at all, despite what the kids said, especially when you didn't look your age. I always would say we were timeless because we were.

It didn't take much longer for them to start boarding us, which was perfect timing. As always, the Travelistas were the first to board with our first-class tickets.

"Do you guys have your shooters?" Dez asked once we were settled on the plane.

"You know I do," I said, opening my Louis Vuitton and showing her the little bottles of alcohol.

"Me too," Roze said. "And after the week I've had, ya girl is going straight to the bar when we land."

"Shit!" Logan exclaimed. "I always forget *something*."

"Don't worry, girl. I brought extras," Dez said.

"Dez, you have always been the lifesaver. Because this was going to be one long-ass flight!"

Logan was right. Ever since I'd met Dez, she'd been a big help to everyone she came into contact with. She'd become the mom of our friend group, always checking on us and making sure we were okay. Even when she was going through her divorce, she made sure everything was tight with our friendship. We of course gave her the same love back, but she was more consistent. Dez was the strong one. She was the glue.

"I have a question for the married ladies on the trip," Dez asked and smiled mischievously at Roze and me.

"Oh, Lord, Ni Ni, she's giving us 'the look.' Should we be nervous?"

"It's just a simple question." Dez shrugged.

"And what is this question?"

"Rings on or off this week?" Once the question was out of her mouth, Roze and I looked at each other.

On vacation, Roze and I sometimes wouldn't wear our wedding rings. Not to cheat on our husbands, but we were on vacation. And that meant there was eye candy everywhere. Just like men liked to flirt and look but not touch, we did too. Roze smiled slowly at me, and I returned it.

"What do you say, Ni Ni?" she asked.

"I say . . . I guess we'll just have to see, won't we?"

It's nothing I'm not used to. . . .

Chapter 8

Roze

So I definitely lied. I thought the first place in Bali that would see me was the bar, but I was wrong. After such a long flight, the first thing that was going to see me was my bed in the villa we'd rented for the week. I'd gotten as much sleep as I could have on the plane, but listen, even the seats in first class were uncomfortable. It was midday when we arrived at the luxurious stay, but my friends had the same thoughts as me. Sleep first, play later.

I wasn't one to get in bed with my outside clothes on, but the moment I stored my luggage and saw the comfy bed, the last thing on my mind was showering or changing my clothes. The only thing I thought to do was put my bonnet over my fresh knotless braids before I got under the covers and closed my eyes. Moments later, I felt a dip in the bed and that forced my eyes back open. It was Imani. She too had her bonnet on, and she made like she was getting ready to go to sleep.

"Do you mind if I nap in here with you? Dez and Logan are already knocked out in Dez's room."

"I don't care. Just don't be trying to feel on me," I said jokingly, and she laughed.

"You wish. You're not my type," she said and set an alarm on her phone. "I'm setting my alarm for eight o'clock so we can get up and go get drinks. That way you can tell me all about what's wrong with you."

"Why do you think something is wrong with me?" I asked, and she made a face.

"You've only been my best friend for over a decade. I definitely know when something isn't right with you. But don't tell me right now. I'm too tired to process anything."

Imani made sure that her phone was right next to her face on the pillow before she got more comfortable. The villa had four bedrooms, but us sleeping in the same room and bed wasn't out of the ordinary. In fact, a lot of times we piled up in one room and passed out wherever we felt like it. In our short stay together, we liked to spend as much time together as possible. I closed my eyes again and soon was fast asleep.

If I had dreams, I had no idea what they were about. What I did know was that when I heard the annoying beeping of Imani's alarm, I groaned. I was glad she grabbed it first because I had half a mind to throw the phone into the wall. I couldn't believe that it was eight o'clock already. It felt like all I'd done was blink. I sat up and rubbed my eyes, trying to force the sleepiness away. Beside me, Imani stretched big with a yawn.

"Damn, that felt short as hell. Let me go get them up and take a shower," she said.

I nodded, and we both got out of bed. She left my room, and I grabbed a cute halter-top dress from my luggage along with some soap so that I could shower. The bathroom connected to my bedroom was so nice, and it had a window inside over the deep tub. The shower was off to the side and was made of brick. There were no curtains or sliding doors. It was all open. I turned on the hot water and stripped off all my clothing. Once I stepped in the steaming shower, I felt complete bliss as the water hit my skin. I could have stayed in there forever, except now that the more I woke up, the more I was ready for a drink.

My mind drifted to my husband, and I wondered how he and the girls were getting along. I'd talked to them once the plane landed and sent my love. However, I couldn't help but think that the trip was the perfect reason and excuse for Isaiah to be sneaky.

After I found the receipt for the hotel and for the flowers in his pocket, I had tried to come up with a game plan to catch him. However, if he really was cheating on me, he was being a smooth criminal. I'd checked both his phone and his computer yet had come up empty. He was either a professional cheater or I'd overreacted about the whole thing. Except I knew I hadn't. But there was nothing that I could do about it all the way in Bali. I'd have to wait until I got home.

I shook those intrusive thoughts away and continued with my shower. I was there to have a good time, and that was what I planned to do. When I was done, I got out and dried off. Before I put the dress over my pear shape, I moisturized my smooth body. With my face I did the bare minimum. A quick brow, some eyelashes, and lip gloss did the job. Once I removed my bonnet and swooped my edges, I was finished and ready. On my way out of the door, I sprayed myself with my favorite Armani perfume and went to find my girls.

Logan was already ready and sitting in the living room on her phone. Her sew-in flowed around her shoulders, and she also wore a cute dress. Ever since I had first met Logan, I always thought she was so pretty. Although she was full black, she had a Native American look about her.

"You look cute," she said when she saw me.

"I was just thinking the same about you," I told her. "Whoever did your install did a fantastic job. You don't think your head will be too hot this week?"

"It's nothing I'm not used to." Logan shrugged. "And when this 'do gets wet, it's going to wave up like the girls in the music videos."

"Come on, water wave!" I said, hyping her up as she whipped her tresses.

"Speaking of come on, I wish those friends of ours would! There's a nightclub not too far from here I thought we could check out. Music, food, beautiful scenery."

"Beautiful scenery?" I asked, making an inquisitive face.

"Yeah. See?" She pulled out her phone and showed me some photos. "It has an inside and outside part, but it's all connected. The inside is more modern, but the outside is nature filled."

"Mm-hmm. I've seen this movie. Right up to the part where we get snatched by some traffickers in the bushes!"

"Stop it, Roze!" Logan laughed. "If it makes you feel any better, we can stay inside."

We were still looking at pictures of the club when Dez and Imani finally joined us. Imani wore a skintight body suit that left nothing to the imagination, and the always-stylish Dez rocked an abstract pair of sheer leggings. Her top reminded me of Aaliyah's in the "Try Again" music video.

"Okay! One time for the bad bitches in the house!" Logan cheered and pulled a bottle of 1942 from behind her.

"Now where the hell did that come from?" Dez raised a brow.

"It was in my checked bag. I figured a little pregaming would be necessary. Who leaves the house sober?"

"Umm, women who are in a foreign country," Dez answered.

"Hello!" I tossed in. "Baby wants us to get kidnapped so bad."

"Well, Lo, I'm with you. Pour me up. Let me get some ice and glasses!" Imani exclaimed and disappeared quickly into the kitchen.

She returned a short time later, carrying four glasses with ice in them. When she handed me mine, I inspected each of the four ice cubes before Logan poured the liquor into it. I wouldn't say that I was a germophobe, but I didn't want to ingest anything I wasn't supposed to either.

"To friendship!" Dez said, holding out her glass, and we all clanked it.

"To friendship!" the rest of us chimed in before taking a swig.

My face instantly twisted up as the liquid hit my chest and trickled down. My shoulders shuddered at the strength of just that one gulp, and around me, I saw that my girls understood my sentiments. If it weren't for the burning sensation in my stomach, I would have laughed at Imani's facial expression. She looked like she'd just bitten into the most sour lemon.

"That shit is too expensive to be so damn nasty." Imani gagged.

"By the time we get our groove back, we won't even flinch at drinking it," Logan said but still set her glass down. "But until then, fuck that nasty shit! I'm ready to go."

We all agreed on the club Logan had suggested, and we left the villa shortly after. The club was close, but not close enough for us to walk. We hailed a ride, and thankfully, the driver spoke English, which made sense since we were near a few resorts. He dropped us off right in front of the restaurant/club and was tipped handsomely. Dez led the way to where the bouncers were checking IDs at the front door, except she walked right past the line of people waiting to get in.

"Dez, the line," I said and pointed, but she waved my words away.

"Girl, I'm not waiting in these shoes. They're about to let us in right now," she told me.

I was shocked, because the Dez I knew was by the book. Maybe the shot of 1942 had gotten to her, but either way I was there for it. I didn't want to wait in my stiletto heels either. As soon as one of the bouncers saw four beautiful black women approaching him, he smiled big. The moment I saw his eyes linger on Logan's booty, I knew we were getting in.

"IDs please," he said in perfect English, and we handed them to him. After looking at them briefly with his flashlight, he gave them back to us, still smiling. "What brings you lovely ladies to Bali?"

"We—"

"It's my birthday," Dez cut Imani off. She was lying, but the charming smile on her face said otherwise. "My girls so graciously made this trip to celebrate with me."

"Nice!" he said, and I kept my face straight.

Her ID clearly stated that her birthday was in December, but I learned a long time ago that they only checked the year and the photo. Nothing else mattered to them. So I went along with my girl because that was what friends did.

"Yup, that's why we came out looking so good tonight," I said, stepping forward and winking at his colleagues behind him. "Probably the sexiest in this place."

"No doubt about it there. My uncle owns it. He'll be very pleased that the four of you came out tonight!" the Asian man said, licking his lips.

"Oh, really? So can this uncle hook me and my girls up or what?" Dez asked, letting her tongue rest on her teeth.

"Go wait by the bar. I'll see what I can do," he said and pulled out a walkie-talkie.

He started speaking a language I didn't understand, and I followed my friends inside. We did what we were told and waited by the bar. Once there, I looked around. The place was jumping. The ambience was something like I'd never experienced. The restaurant seamlessly blended into a night club, and the aroma from the food made me want some expeditiously. But then again, the DJ was on point, and my body wanted to go dance.

When we came to Bali the last time, it was a peaceful trip filled with a lot of nature and bonding, so it was quite the surprise to see that they got down like that.

"Your birthday, bitch?" I heard Logan say to Dez over the music.

I turned back to see a smug smirk on Dez's face as she ordered us all drinks. "Are you mad I lied?" she asked.

"No, it's just first you're cutting in line, and then you lie about it being your birthday. I've just never seen this side of you before."

"I'm on vacation, bitch! I just want to enjoy myself," Dez said, giving the bartender some cash and handing us all the same red drink. "Y'all are going to love this!"

"What is it?" I asked, sniffing the fruity drink.

"I don't know. I just told her to make us something we'd love!" Dez laughed.

Before I could say anything else, a man wearing a suit approached us and motioned for us to follow him to VIP. When we got to the spacious section, I was blown away by the arrangement that was put together for us. I knew it was for us because in the middle of the chilled bottles and food garnishes, on a glass table was a two-tiered cake that said "Happy Birthday." Imani made an impressed expression with her face and sat down on the cushioned seat. I sat right next to her and set the red

questionable drink in my hand on the table. The
man turned to Dez and kissed her hand softly.

"I hope this is to the birthday girl's liking," he
said.

"It is, but wow. You didn't have to go to all this
trouble," she told him.

"The boss insisted."

"And where is he if you don't mind me asking?"

"Up there," he said and pointed to a section on a
higher level in the club.

We all looked up, and there was an Asian man
waving down at us. I was taken aback because
he didn't look to be much older than us. He must
have been rolling in dough in order to own a place
like that. I wanted to tell Dez to make sure she got
his contact information before we left, but when I
looked at her, it seemed like she already had that
on her mind. The way she was smiling up at the
man a person would have thought the two knew
each other, but that wasn't possible. I picked up
one of the bottles and held it in the air.

"To the birthday girl! Now let's get this party
started!"

Whatever it takes. . . .

Chapter 9

Dez

Now normally I liked to tell the truth or something close to it. But that night I wanted to live it up like there was no tomorrow. Originally, telling the bouncer that it was my birthday was just meant to get us in the club for free. I had no idea that it would get us treated like royalty for the night. My eyes almost popped out of their sockets when I saw the section made for us. I almost felt bad for lying, but when the man pointed at who was behind it all, I understood.

My girls and I drank, laughed, and danced our hearts out. It was like we were back at our first year of college. Back then we, for lack of a better phrase, were hot girls. If there was a party, we were there shaking what our mamas gave us. It was good to see that none of us had lost it. In the midst of it all, I was looking for a window of opportunity to sneak away, and when one wasn't presented, I decided to tap Imani on her arm. She turned to face me, smiling and out of breath. I couldn't help but laugh. Seeing them so happy did something to my heart.

"I'm going to be right back," I said into her ear.

"Uh-uh. You know we do the buddy system. Let me grab my purse. I'll come with you."

"No, I'll be all right. I swear. I'm just going to go tell the owner thanks for everything."

"Ohhh." Imani gave me a knowing look. "You wearing panties? If you are, come over here and take them off. Nobody's looking. I'll put them in my purse for you."

"Stop it!" I laughed and moved my arm away from her before she could drag me to some dark corner. "It's nothing like that. I just want to say thank you. I'll text you to let you know I'm safe. And plus, you know I don't wear panties, bitch."

I winked as I walked off and felt a sting as she slapped my bottom. I was smiling all the way to the elevator that went to the second level of the club. Once up there, I didn't exactly know where I was going, but I went in the direction of where I thought the section was. I figured I'd found it when I saw two tinted glass double doors and four muscular men standing outside of it. As I approached, I found myself fixing up my hair with my fingers.

"Can we help you?" one of the guards asked me when I got to the doors.

"Yes, I um, wanted to speak with the owner." The men chuckled and looked at each other like what I'd just asked was funny. "Is something wrong?"

"Andrew wasn't expecting any entertainment tonight," the same man spoke.

"Enter . . . what? I'm not a whore. Just please go and tell him I'm here to see him."

"Listen, woman, how about you go back downstairs and enjoy yourself like the other guests, huh?" He made like he was about to take a step toward me, but then the door behind them opened.

Standing there was the man who had waved down to us from his section and who the security guard had referred to as Andrew. However, I'd come to know him as Andy. His smile said it all when he saw me standing there, and I was sure mine was just as big.

"Desiree," he finally said and opened his arms wide.

"Andy."

I fell into his arms and allowed him to hold me for more than a few seconds. When we finally broke away from each other, the men standing around us looked bewildered. But I didn't care. There was a fire of joy lit inside of me at that moment that no one could put out.

"Come in and have a drink with me," he said, gesturing for me to follow him.

I did, but I made sure to flick off the guard who was giving me a hard time. It was childish, but the buzz I had made me not care. Once the door was shut behind me, I saw that his section was much larger than ours. In fact, he had his own bar and bartender up there. Andy took me to a seat on the side away from all of his guests and sat beside me. His hands found mine, and he just looked at me in awe. He was still as handsome as the day I'd met him. Andy was in his early forties but had the muscular body of a man half his age. Also, he drank his water and kept his hair dyed black, so if you didn't know his age, it would be hard to guess.

"So it's your birthday, huh? I thought that was in December," he said knowingly, and I burst out laughing so hard.

"It *is* in December, but the line outside was long, so I improvised," I told him with a shrug of one shoulder. "I was so shocked when I saw you waving at us I almost shit myself."

"I just couldn't believe my eyes when it was you standing there. I never thought that I'd see you again."

"Me either, but I think that was kind of the point," I told him shyly.

I had no idea why I was being shy. In another lifetime, Andy and I might have ended up together. However, I'd ended up finding something I didn't know I needed on that vacation. Andy and I lost touch after.

"The last time I saw you, you told me you were living in the States, right? When did you move to Bali?" I asked curiously.

"After you and I met actually. My mother has always been on my back about visiting our homeland, but it wasn't until you spoke so highly of it that I decided to make the trip. And well, I never left. I started a few businesses and have been doing quite well for myself."

"I see!" I said and ran my hands down the fine fabric of his suit jacket. "Wow. I'm so happy for you."

"Thank you. What about you? Are you still the best teacher in the universe?"

"You could say that." I smiled. "There have been a few changes in my life."

"You got remarried?"

"No, not yet."

"You're thinking about it?"

"Maybe. However, I must admit that I didn't know the toll my ex-husband left on me. I haven't been close to another man since."

"Such a shame. You are still the most beautiful woman I've ever laid eyes on."

"Don't butter me up. You know I won't tire of hearing that," I told him, and he laughed.

"How have you been, after the island? We didn't speak after."

"I think that was the point," I said with a small smile. "But to answer your question, things are just . . . different now."

"How so?"

"They just are."

There was a small silence between us. I didn't want to unveil to him that I was dying and ruin the mood. Plus, I didn't even know how I would say it. But lucky for me, I didn't have to. Suddenly Andy gazed deeply into my eyes and spoke in a serious tone.

"I know it's been a while since we last saw each other or spoke, but seeing you standing there with your friends, it felt like seeing fireworks for the first time. I know it sounds crazy, but I don't want to lose you again. I'll open a club wherever you're at so we can see each other often. Whatever it takes."

"Whatever it takes," I repeated him and looked at the sincerity of his expression. I pulled my hands away and kissed him on his cheek. "How nice it must be to be so rich that you can plan your life with somebody so quickly. I just came up here to say hi and thank you. For everything."

"Wait, Desiree. Are you seeing someone else?" His words held sadness, and all I could do was touch his face with my palm briefly.

"Goodbye, Andy."

I stood up and walked away from him before he could try to talk me into staying. I'd done well to avoid his question. My love life was one I'd decided to keep to myself. Not even my girls knew about what I had going on. To my surprise, on my way out, I ran right into my friends, who were in the middle of a verbal altercation with the security.

"There she is!" Logan exclaimed and pointed at me.

"Oh, my God, Dez. You had us scared as hell! You said you were going to text me and tell me you were okay!" Roze exclaimed.

"I'm sorry. I forgot."

"You forgot? Girl, you almost got these big-ass men fucked up! We thought they'd done something to you when you didn't text or come back. Are you okay?"

Seeing my friends about to pounce on four men twice their sizes in my honor made me forget about my sad goodbye to Andy. Imani had been in the middle of swinging her crossbody, and Logan still had one of her hands balled into a fist. I grinned at them and just shook my head.

"Well, as you guys can see, I'm alive and well. Let's go before they kick us out of here." I pushed them away from the doors and back toward the elevator.

If he isn't getting it from me, then who? . . .

Chapter 10

Logan

"Mmm!"

It was my own moan that woke me out of my sleep. I had an out-of-this-world headache, and I was still fully dressed in my outfit from the night before, shoes included. I didn't remember much after we got back from the club except that we had a few more shots of 1942 and rapped along to a few of Boosie's songs. After that it was a blur. Still, somehow I'd managed to make it to my bed, but that was literally how far I got. I was lying on top of my covers on my back, staring at the overhead fan spinning. That was a bad idea, because suddenly I felt an overwhelming sensation to puke.

I jumped up from the bed and ran to the bathroom connected to my room. Well, more like stumbled. Either way I made it just in time to spill all of my insides into the toilet. It smelled like a mixture of wings and liquor. Gross. I gagged a few more times, but nothing else came out.

"Whew!" I breathed, pushing away from the toilet and resting my back on the wall behind me.

Unfastening the clasp on my heels, I took the shoes off and tossed them back into the bedroom. The nauseated feeling was subsiding, and while it did, I got my breathing under control. The last time I was that drunk I was at a Nicki Minaj concert. I told myself back then I would never let that happen again, but obviously I'd lied to myself. There I was sitting on the floor, looking like five women had whooped my ass.

"Lo?" The voice belonged to Imani. I couldn't find the energy to respond, but I knew she would eventually find me. She did. "Oh, my God, Logan! Are you okay? Do you need a doctor?"

Imani, who was a ray of sunshine in her satin nightgown and floral kimono, knelt beside me and put a hand to my forehead. She genuinely looked concerned at the state I was in.

"Bitch, I'm not dying. I'm hungover! And it's all your fault."

"My fault? You're the one who brought the 1942!"

"I know, but blaming the way I feel on somebody else just seems like the right thing to do right now. Because admitting to myself I did this sounds so wrong."

"Girl, get your drunk ass up. The cooks came and made us breakfast. You need some grease in your stomach. Come on. Can you shower? You smell like puke."

"I think so."

She helped me up and had me sit on the toilet while she started my water. After that, she left the room and returned minutes later with a water bottle. And that wasn't all she had with her. Dez and Roze entered the bathroom close behind her. They too were wearing matching satin nightgowns and kimonos.

"Mmm, Mani told us you were in here still drunk. Here. Eat this for now," Roze said and held a piece of bacon to my mouth.

I gobbled it down, and it was delicious. Not only that, but it gave me the small boost of energy I needed to take a shower. I went to undress, but my girls stepped in to help me. Once I was completely naked, Dez helped me in the shower while Imani lathered a few loofas I'd brought. It wasn't the first time my friends had seen me naked in the shower, but it was the first time they bathed me. I was so grateful to them in that moment because I was using all of my energy to just stand up. Once they were finished, I cleaned my own private areas and rinsed off. Dez helped me back out and dry off while Roze went and got my nightgown that matched theirs.

"I made these months ago," Imani said to me as I put lotion on my body. "I thought today would be the perfect time to wear them. They're one of a kind because I embroidered all of our names in the bustlines."

The gowns were indeed beautiful. They were the color of champagne, and the floral kimonos were the same color, just sheer. I'd always felt that Imani had done the right thing by leaving the world of law and following her dream of not only being a seamstress, but a fashion designer. She used to keep us all flyer than all of the girls in college with her one-of-a-kind pieces.

"Thank you," I said and took the gown from her. After I put it and the kimono on, I looked at myself in the mirror. My hair still was flawless, and I didn't look as messed up in the face. I smiled. "Thank you, guys, for taking care of me. For *always* taking care of me."

"You know we're going to make sure our girl is straight," Dez said and then pointed out of the bathroom. "Okay, now let's go eat because my stomach is growling something vicious!"

I was with her on that. I'd thrown up everything in my stomach, and that little piece of bacon Roze gave me could sure use some company. We all filed into the kitchen and sat down at the circular table after loading our plates. The cooks had come and cooked all of our favorite dishes, and it smelled amazing. Not to mention that a beautiful view was paired with our meal. Our villa overlooked our private pool, and past that was a beautiful forest area. It was so peaceful that I could stay there all day.

"So, ladies, I was thinking we'd use today to catch up since we weren't able to yesterday," Dez said, seemingly reading my mind.

"I'm down. I definitely need a day to recuperate from this hangover," I agreed. "Plus, I need to get all up in you heffas' business."

"We're going to get to their business soon enough. But first I'm curious about yours with Nathan," Dez asked, cutting a piece of her French toast. "Did my bedroom advice work?"

"Hold on, since when does Miss Freak Nik need bedroom advice?" Imani asked, intrigued.

"Girl, you know I don't. It's Nathan," I sighed and rolled my eyes. "He's so fine and sweet, but he's a minute man!"

"No!" Roze and Imani gasped.

"Yes. I tell you no lies. At this big age, he cannot hold his nut back. I'm so sexually frustrated that last night I didn't know if I would have beaten that security guard up or let him beat this pussy up, do you hear me?"

We all laughed loudly. Imani put up a finger as she got herself together. "So have you tried anything to boost his stamina?" she asked.

"Well, Dez came up with the idea of doing it in a pitch-black room."

"Mm, yup, that's a good idea. Because he probably gets distracted by all the thickness. Did it work?"

"No! And you know what makes me more upset? As a man you *know* when your woman isn't sexually satisfied, and with Nathan I told him from the beginning that I'm a freak. So the fact that he's a quick pumper *and* he doesn't do anything to ensure that I get mine too really grinds my gears!"

"I don't even know what to say. I am outdone," Roze said, shaking her head.

"Yeah, Lo, I'm sorry. I thought that would help," Dez added. "What are you going to do?"

"I don't know. He's truly the best guy I've ever dated, and I don't want to throw it away behind something that can be fixed."

"But what if it can't? You'll just be putting yourself in the line of fire to fall for temptation and break that man's heart. I say you leave his ass."

"Roze!" Dez exclaimed.

"What? We all know Lo has a high sex drive. If he's not fucking her the way she needs to be fucked, she's going to find it elsewhere. Why break his heart when you can just leave?"

"How about we exhaust all options before we tell our friend to leave a good man?"

"Well, do that with her, not with me. Because I'm leaving Isaiah's ass."

"What?" Imani and I asked in unison.

Dez didn't seem surprised at Roze's admission, which didn't shock me. We all called her first at the slightest inconvenience in our lives. Roze pursed her lips and stabbed at a grape on her plate.

"Y'all heard me. I'm leaving his no-good ass."

"But why? You've been together for so long, and the girls would be devastated!" I said.

"How about you ask him if he was thinking about our daughters when he was sneaking around with his skank?"

"Isaiah's cheating?" Imani asked with her hand to her chest.

"I know he is. I found receipts for flowers and room service for two. That lying bastard told me he was doing business in Savannah, but the hotel receipt said Buckhead."

"Girl, that doesn't mean he's cheating," I said. "You need more proof than that."

"What more proof can I get? That says it all!"

"Go up to the hotel and ask for yourself. Tell them your husband left something in the room." I stopped talking, and Roze looked confused.

"And then what?"

"Nothing. The looks on people at the front desk's faces will tell you all you need to know. If he went there once with a woman, he's comfortable, which meant he's probably been there more than once."

"You sound like you've done this before," Dez teased.

"Y'all know I had my share of 'ain't shit' men," I said. "You remember when I caught two-timing Jerome in *my* car with his side chick? That bastard really dropped me off at work and picked her up!"

"Well, the first mistake was letting him take your car in the first place."

"Dez, don't make me get you. Hungover and all," I warned through my giggle.

"Well, speaking of 'ain't shit' men, I guess it's my turn to have the floor," Imani sighed. "I think Kevin is cheating too."

I found myself groaning as I ate my food. Isaiah I could almost believe was having an affair. Only because, although he and Roze had grown together, over time they'd grown apart. As he got more successful, so did she. In his warped version of reality, he thought Roze would give up her businesswoman dreams. The fact that she wouldn't had caused fights over the past few years. I knew because there were times she'd called me, crying after them. That could have hyped Isaiah to step out and find a less ambitious woman to fuel his ego. I hoped not, but it was worth Roze looking into.

However, Kevin, on the other hand? That man worshipped the ground Imani walked on. I prayed my husband would support me the way he had her. Not only did he have her back when she quit her job, but he relocated to a place where her business would thrive. They were best friends as well as partners. So him cheating was something I just couldn't believe.

"Kevin wouldn't cheat on you." I shook my head in disbelief.

"How can you be so sure?"

"First tell us why you think he's cheating."

"Every time we go out, I'm picking up the bill because he conveniently leaves his wallet at home."

"Okay, maybe he really is leaving his wallet at home."

"Ha! No. Kevin is one of the most responsible people I know. So that *and* the fact that I've been covering most of the bills is letting me know something is going on."

"Maybe he's stashing money away for a divorce."

"Roze!" Dez exclaimed her way again.

"I'm sorry, y'all. I'm just being a Debbie Downer right now. I'm going to shut up and let y'all talk." Roze shook her head sadly.

I felt for her, but I was focused on Imani's nonsense in that moment. "Is that all?" I asked.

"I'm telling you guys something isn't right. When you've been with and lived with someone as long as I have Kevin, you know when something is amiss. And something isn't right. And did I mention, before the morning of my flight, we hadn't had sex in weeks."

"Weeks?" I raised my brow.

"Yes! And Kevin is a sex machine. He needs it at least ten times a week to function. So if he isn't getting it from me, then who?"

"I don't know. Dez, what do you think?" I asked, and Dez shrugged her shoulders.

"I think both of them are crazy. Whenever there's a problem in a marriage, another woman isn't always the reason why. Take my lying-ass, scheming ex-husband for example. We grew apart."

"Yeah, you catching him stealing and hiding money in the walls of your old house had nothing to do with it. How much was it again?" Roze stated.

"I thought you said you were going to be quiet," Dez said, shooting her a look. Roze made a motion like she was zipping her lips shut and leaned back in her chair. Dez sighed and shook her head. "That is a big part of the reason I divorced Caleb. His illegal dealings in the courtroom made me realize that I had no clue who I was married to. He wasn't the person I met in college. Or maybe he was and just hid that side of him well. Either way, we were no longer a match, and I did what I needed to do. But *you* ladies have situations way different from mine. They can work. Listen to your husbands and what they want."

"We do! I mean, I do anyways," Imani said, and Dez shook her head again.

"I'm not saying listen to their words. Listen to their *lives*. Men aren't good with telling you what they want verbally, but if you pay close enough attention, they'll tell you with their moves. Pay attention."

"And this is exactly why you're our free counselor," I joked. "But enough about us. We'll figure this shit out one way or another. What's new with you? I swear you keep your business locked tighter than Fort Knox."

"That's because there is no business to tell," Dez said, looking down at the hashbrowns on her plate.

"You haven't been dating?"

"Nope," she said with a straight face.

"No dick at *all*?"

"Nope. And I'm just fine with it."

"Oh, hell no, bitch. Roze? Imani? You know what this means, right?"

"We have to get her laid!" Imani shouted, and we all fell into a fit of giggles.

Flattery will get you everywhere with me. . . .

Chapter 11

Imani

Fun wasn't the word to describe the time I'd been having with my girls. It was like we were back in our early twenties living carefree again. In fact, being with them was almost enough to make me forget about my problems at home. Almost. Our week together was quickly coming to an end, and before I knew it, we only had two more days in Bali. That day we planned to have some fun in the sun and go do water activities. However, there was one thing I needed to do before we left.

"Roze, tell them I'll be right there!" I called after putting sunscreen all over my body.

"Okay, but hurry up!"

And I knew she meant it. Water activities were our favorite and something we usually saved for the last day. Dez wanted to change that tradition this trip though, which was fine with me. I couldn't wait to wear my lime green bikini with the matching crocheted cover-up bottoms. I stared at my reflection in the mirror and admired all of my curves. Once I was all the way together, I grabbed my phone and sat down on the bed.

Although I'd checked in a few times, I hadn't checked the camera footage from back home since I'd been on vacation. So that meant if Kevin was doing something he didn't have any business doing, he'd had all the time in the world. I pulled up the surveillance app and first clicked on the watch live option. After a few seconds I realized that nobody was home, so I watched all of the prior footage. There were no strangers coming in and out of the house, but I did notice something strange.

The last few nights Kevin was coming home from work and leaving again shortly after. That wouldn't have alarmed me if he weren't dressed in what I would consider club attire: silk shirts, Cartier shades, and his favorite jewelry. Most wouldn't think much of that. What man wouldn't take the time to go out and have man time when his wife was gone? But Kevin wasn't the typical man. The only friends he had were his colleagues from work, and none of them dressed like they were fresh off the cover of *GQ*. And I could bet money that he had smelled delicious, too. From experience, I knew that the only time a man took the time to look that good was when women were involved. I paused the screen and zoomed in on his hands. My heart skipped a beat when I saw that, of all the jewelry Kevin was wearing, his wedding ring was missing. Wow.

"I should have put a camera in his damn car," I said to myself, clicking out of the app.

"Damn, you aren't ready yet? I can't hold those hyenas off any longer. They are ready to go! What's taking you so long?"

Roze walked into my bedroom and lightly hit me on my shoulder. I hadn't realized how much time had gone by. I hopped up and grabbed my sun hat and beach bag so we could go.

"My bad, girl. I'm ready."

"Ohh, girl, that swimsuit is cute! Okay, ass poking!" Roze slapped my bottom as I passed.

"You know it's healthy." I twerked playfully.

I followed her to where Dez and Logan were waiting for us outside. Our driver was already there with a van, and when Roze and I exited the house, we all loaded up inside. My friends were talking and laughing among each other on the way to our destination, but me? I was trying to force myself to be present so that I could fight the urge to call Kevin. I wanted to know where the hell he was going at that time of night and why he was coming back so late. I wanted to know why he had to wait for me to go out of town to go out like that. I couldn't remember the last time he and I had a night on the town. When we first got together, we used to go out all the time. Now something else clearly had his attention. I found myself slipping my wedding ring off and putting it into my bag.

"Oh, so that's what we're doing today?" Logan asked, and when I looked up, she was staring at me.

"I just don't want to lose it in the water." I smirked at her.

"Un-huh, and I'm sure it has nothing to do with you thinking Kevin is cheating."

"Nope. Sure doesn't. But since you brought it up, if that motherfucker can have some fun, why can't I?"

"And I concur," Roze said and slid her wedding ring off too. "If I have to go home and face the reality that my marriage is blowing up in my face, I'm going to enjoy the hell out of myself these last few days."

"Good, because I have a surprise for you ladies," Dez said, grinning devilishly as we pulled into a boarding dock.

She pointed outside of the window toward a beautiful white yacht. Next to it were jet skis and a parasailing chute. That wasn't all that was waiting for us though. On the yacht, waving at us were four of the sexiest island men I'd ever laid eyes on. Their muscles were busting out of their T-shirts, and they all wore swim trunks. That led me to believe that they planned on going swimming.

"Are they coming with us?" I asked.

"They aren't on our yacht for nothing. I thought it would be fun for us to have some eye candy."

"Where did you meet these guys?" Logan asked.

"Last night at dinner while you guys were on the dance floor, I overheard them say their family owns a boat. I told them we were doing water activities today, and they invited us," Dez said like it was nothing.

The night before was a pleasant blur. We'd gone out again and had a ball. I briefly remembered a time where Dez wasn't with us. That must have been what she was talking about.

"I don't know. Getting on a boat with strangers doesn't seem like the smartest thing to do," Roze said, making a distrusting face.

"Girl, what's the difference between this and getting on the boat of a scuba instructor? You think those people are really professionals? No!" Dez rolled her eyes and got out of the van.

"How old are they?" I asked, glancing at the men again.

"Tomas, the one with the short, spiky hair, is twenty-five. He's the one who invited us, and he's mine, so don't get any ideas." Dez pointed her finger at each one of us.

"Twenty-five?" Roze exclaimed. "Lawd, you got us out here robbing the cradle!"

"I thought you wanted to live a little. Come on!"

Roze hesitated, but eventually she got out of the car. Logan was next and then me. Once again, I was taken aback by Dez's daredevil behavior. Especially in that moment. Usually it was Roze who wanted to do some off-the-rocker stuff, not Dez. So for Roze to be the skeptical one said a lot. Still, we found ourselves walking toward the yacht.

"Hey, Tomas! These are my friends!" Dez called, and they rushed to help us on board.

One of them wore his hair in two long French braids and had sharks on his swim trunks. His olive skin was tanned, and he had a dazzling white smile. He grabbed my bag and my hand so that I could step on board with no issue.

The yacht was huge like the ones I used to watch in music videos. The captain's deck was raised from the main deck, and there was a sitting area and bar inside. I could see stairs that led to a lower level, but until I got a feel for these men, I wouldn't be going anywhere that would be difficult to get out of. I suspiciously eyed the man who'd helped me down, and he laughed.

"Hi, I'm Dominic. It's nice to meet you," he introduced himself in a deep voice, and his brown eyes twinkled as he spoke to me.

"I'm Imani. Nice to meet you too."

"Would you like to sit?" He made a gesture to the inside of the yacht.

"Umm." I looked around and saw there was a sitting area where we were at. "Here is fine."

"No worries. I understand. You just met me, but I promise I'm not a crazy person or anything like that."

"I'll be the judge of that," I said, and we sat side by side. "So how old are you, and are you from here?"

"I'm twenty-eight," he answered. "What about you?"

"Oop, didn't your mother ever teach you that it's bad to ask a woman her age? How old do I look?"

"Mid-twenties."

"And we're going to just go with that, because you might not know it, but black doesn't crack. Are you from around here?"

"No. My younger brother Tomas over there and I are here visiting family. As well as our cousins David"—he pointed at the man with Logan—"and Henry." He pointed at the man with Roze. "This is our family's dock."

"So you're from the States?"

"I guess you can say that. I travel a lot. But in all of my travels, never have I come across a woman as beautiful as you."

"Flattery will get you everywhere with me," I said with a giggle.

I had to admit, he didn't give me creep vibes. Nor did I feel bad as a married woman for sitting so close to him. I was on vacation and deserved to have some eye candy. And ooh, some hand candy, too. Beside me, Dominic pulled his shirt over his head, and the sun glistened off of his pecks. I found myself grinning in the direction of Logan, who was silently giving me the thumbs-up sign behind her new friend's back. Above us, Dez winked from the captain's deck and pointed at the jet skis.

"Don't get too comfortable now because it's time to get in the water!"

Trust me, everything that glitters isn't gold. . . .

Chapter 12

Logan

I didn't know whether to think Dez was off her rocker for hooking us up with these young boys we didn't know or to thank her. Because I definitely needed some hot excitement in my life. And David was proving to be just that. His whole chest was covered in tattoos, and he wore his hair cut short and faded on the sides. I was even feeling the crisp lineup he had going on. He was fine as hell, that was for sure. I didn't even care that he was younger than me. Hell, if Stella could get her groove back, so could I.

My arms wrapped around his waist as we sped over the waves on one of the jet skis. As I squealed in joy, I couldn't help but to cop a few feels of his bare upper half. He was solid, and I couldn't help but to wonder how strong he was. As it happened, I didn't have to wonder about that for much longer. Right at that moment, David hit a wave so powerful that it knocked both of us off of the jet ski.

"Oh, my God, Logan!"

I couldn't tell which one of my friends had just shouted for me. I was too busy flailing around, trying to stay above water. Although it was clear, there was still only so far my eyes could see under me. I had terrible visions of Jaws coming and feasting on me.

David swam over and grabbed on to me, holding firm. He swam with me in tow all the way back to the jet ski and hoisted me up like I was but a hundred pounds. When he climbed on, I wrapped my arms tightly around his waist and rested my head on his back.

"Okay, that killed it for me! I am so over this," I said.

"Are you ready to go back to the boat already?" he asked.

"Yes! After that I need a drink. You do have drinks, don't you?"

"At the bar on the yacht. What about your friends?"

I turned my head to look at them and saw that they were having a good time on the water. No need to make them suffer because I was over it. "They seem to be getting along okay without me. Plus, I need to use the little girls' room."

He nodded and turned the jet ski in the direction of the yacht. Once there, he helped me on board and pointed me in the direction of the bathroom. I really didn't have to go. I just wanted to make sure the lace on my install was still glued down firmly. After making sure I was still eye candy, I made my way out to the bar. David was already there with an unopened bottle of champagne and two empty glasses.

"I wanted to wait for you to pour it. You know how things are in this climate."

He gave me a lighthearted smile, but I knew he was serious. And I couldn't blame him. The same way we were being cautious with them I was sure they were being with us. I grabbed a glass and held it out to him after he popped open the bottle so he could pour me some. I wasn't a fan of champagne, but it would have to do. We sat down together on one of the white couches, and I downed the entire glass in record time. The sooner I felt the buzz, the better.

"So tell me more about yourself, Logan. Besides the fact that you like to drink."

I had to laugh because with the way I had gulped that champagne, I must have looked like an alcoholic. I definitely wasn't. "I'm sorry. I guess maybe I'm a little nervous."

"Nervous about what? Me?" he asked innocently.

That wasn't it. Or maybe it was. Something about being so close to him was making my stomach do flips. The last time that happened I was sexually frustrated at a frat party and ended up sleeping with two frat brothers. And right then with David, I knew my stomach was flipping for the very same reason. Nate had sent me on vacation hornier than ever, and right then David was looking like the perfect person to take my frustration out on.

"So?" he asked, interrupting my unsavory thoughts.

"Huh?"

"You're supposed to be telling me more about you."

"Oh, well, what do you want to know?"

"Whatever you're comfortable telling me."

"Okay, um, I'm from Atlanta, but I moved to New York to pursue my dreams of being an artist."

"And how is that going for you?"

"It's . . . going," I said with a laugh. "I mean, I do well and can sell my work at a nice price point. It's just . . . I don't know. I guess I thought my dream would have taken off by now. I still work a regular job that I hate, and my friends help me out more than I like. You know, I don't know why I'm telling you all of this. I'm sorry."

I put my hand over my face the moment I realized I was rambling. I hated oversharing when I didn't have to. David gently lowered my hand and offered me a kind smile.

"You don't have to be embarrassed. I should be the one embarrassed. All of this is my family's. I've never had to work hard for anything in my life."

"Want to trade?" I joked.

"Trust me, everything that glitters isn't gold."

"You sure about that?" I asked, biting my lip.

There it was. My buzz had finally kicked in, and it made him seem even sexier than he was already. Water still trickled from his hair and fell as little droplets onto his broad shoulders. My eyes traveled from his slanted brown eyes to his full pink lips.

"Since you aren't judging me, can I tell you something else, David?"

"Sure."

"I have a boyfriend at home."

"Oh! I'm sorry. Have I offended you? I know most guys don't care, but I believe in karma, man." He made to move away from me, but I grabbed his hand to stop him.

"You haven't offended me at all. In fact, you reminded me of an itch I have."

"An itch?"

"Yes. One my boyfriend can't seem to scratch. And I *need* it scratched. Can you help me?"

I batted my lashes at him because fuck karma. I wanted him. A slow smile crept on his face when he understood what I was saying. He quickly glanced over his shoulder to see if anyone was coming, but I knew we had more than enough time. I pulled my swimsuit top down so when he turned back to face me, he was staring right at my brown breasts. His eyes grew wide, and I motioned with my finger for him to come closer.

His lips found mine, and with the way he kissed me, I felt like I was in a romance movie. A forbidden romance movie. His hands fondled my breasts and pinched my nipples as our tongues danced.

"Mmm," I moaned into his mouth.

"Open," he instructed when he broke our kiss.

I didn't know what he meant until he pulled my swim bottoms off and opened my legs. He had the perfect view of my fat cat, and he wasted no time diving in headfirst. I relaxed my body as he sucked my clit like it was a pacifier, and I relished the feeling of pleasure. His tongue worked magic on my pussy until I felt my love button swell up.

My first orgasm came fast and took a lot of energy from me. But not so much that I wasn't hungry for more. When David finally came up for air, my juices were dripping from his chin. I pushed him back and straddled him. I needed some dick, and I needed it badly. The last thing on my mind was asking if he had protection.

David slid his trunks down just enough to pull his manhood out, and I was definitely impressed by the size. He was so excited his breathing was rigid, and his hand was shaky. But he managed to position the tip against my opening, and I slid down on his thick member. He awakened all of the sensations in my vaginal canal, and I bit my lip at how amazing it felt. David grabbed handfuls of my round bottom and guided me up and down. He slid in and out of me, and soon all that could be heard were my moans of ecstasy. As I bounced on him, his head rolled back, and his face twisted in bliss. Every time I plopped down, his curved tip hit my G-spot, and I knew it wouldn't be long until I came again. However, David surprised me before I could. He pushed me off of him and bent me over on the couch.

I heard a spitting sound and felt liquid trickle down my crack. When he slid back into my pussy, I felt the sting of him shoving his thumb in my ass. I didn't know whether to moan or to shout in pain. Oh, but it felt so good. He thrust into me so powerfully I had no choice but to bury my head into a couch pillow. The love cries I spoke were muffled, which was a good thing because I probably wasn't making any sense anyways. All I could do was keep my back arched and let him have his way with me. My orgasm snuck up on me, and my legs quivered as a gush of juices spilled out onto his third leg.

"Shit, girl, I'm coming. *Ohhh,* I'm coming!" he shouted right before he pulled out.

He massaged the semen out and let it shoot onto my bare ass. After I caught my breath, I grabbed my swimsuit bottoms and went to the bathroom to wipe myself clean. When I looked into the mirror that time, I had a big smile on my face. David didn't even know how happy he had made me or how badly I really needed that. I still cared about Nate, but when a girl needed her back blown out, she needed her back blown out!

"What About Your Friends"

Chapter 13

Dez

Hiding my sickness from my friends was something I'd worried about prior to our trip. But it actually proved to be easier than I thought. However, being able to hide it didn't change the fact that I still was. Sick, that is. I felt it every day during our vacation even when I pretended I didn't. The nausea was easy to hide because I could just say it was from the alcohol. My tiredness didn't take much to mask because we all slept a lot. The sadness I felt didn't hit me until our final full day together. It wasn't hard to hide that either, since our last day together was usually a tearjerker.

That morning we got up just like we had the other days and went to the kitchen for breakfast. Our cooks had definitely shown out the whole week by making our favorite dishes. I was happy I thought to book them that time around. I didn't mind trying other cultures' food, but sometimes a person just wanted to stick to what they knew. Roze and Imani were already at the table eating when I got to the kitchen.

"Good morning, ladies," I greeted them as I fixed myself a plate of shrimp and grits. "After yesterday I'm surprised any of us are up this early."

"Whew! What a time!" Roze smiled, reminiscing. "Handsome men and water play are always a good mix. And it felt even better without someone asking questions about my family. I love my girls, but it felt good being an individual."

"Oh, I forgot you dumped the ring! How'd that go for you?" I asked.

"I mean, y'all were there the whole time, and you know he didn't even get to first base. But it felt good being desired, you know? I don't know the last time Isaiah made me feel *anything*."

"I definitely understand that. I think we all enjoyed ourselves. And watching Lo fall off that jet ski was hilarious!" Imani added, laughing hysterically.

"Hey, not nice," I said, pointing at her.

I set my plate of food on the table and sat down with them. My words didn't stop Imani from laughing, and playing the memory back in my head, I had to laugh too. I still didn't know how Logan and David flipped over like that in the water. I was glad my girl was okay, but after that, she'd had enough. We didn't see her again until after we were done parasailing.

"Good morning!" The sing-song voice interrupted our laughter.

Logan had finally come to join us. She seemed to float as she walked around the kitchen, and she had a certain glow about her. Frozen on her face was a small smile like one on a child when they had done something no one else knew. She made her plate and joined us, humming to herself.

"We were just talking about you," Imani said, trying to stifle her laugh.

"Oh, really? What about me?"

"Girl, she is over there cracking up at how you flipped off that jet ski!" Roze said, busting Imani out.

"That's all right. She can laugh her heart out. I'm happy it happened. It gave me a reason to have some alone time with David."

There was something about the way she said it. Not only that, but the matter-of-fact face that she paired with it. I raised a brow as I watched her take a few bites of toast. I couldn't let it go. "What's that supposed to mean? *Alone time?*"

"I fucked him," she said with a shrug.

Across from me, Roze choked on her orange juice. Imani's fork hit her plate, and my fingers went to my lips. Logan, on the other hand, didn't miss a beat. She continued eating like she hadn't just dropped that bomb on us.

"You did what?" I asked.

"I fucked him," she repeated but then made a thoughtful face and tapped her chin. "Actually, I think he fucked me. I came so hard. Whew! I needed that."

"But what about Nathan?" Roze asked.

"What about him? Last time I checked we weren't married."

"Yeah, but don't you at least feel a little bad?"

"No," Logan said at first, but then she rolled her eyes. "Okay, maybe a little. But I was horny! Like super horny! I couldn't pass up an opportunity like that. For what? So I can go back home and continue being unsatisfied?"

"I still don't think it's right."

"Says the woman who took her wedding ring off."

"I looked. I didn't touch," Roze shot back.

"Did you at least get his number?" Imani asked, and Logan shook her head.

"I surely did not. I hit and quit. Nothing more, nothing less!"

Roze and Imani looked at our friend in wonder. Out of all of us, Logan had always been the more promiscuous one. She could detach feelings from sex unlike any woman I'd ever met. She would get her rocks off, and that was that. Up until recently, it was something I'd always admired about her and wanted to try. So I did.

"What if there were a place where that's all you did? Hit and quit, I mean?" I heard myself asking.

"There is a place. Lo just proved it with her fast ass," Imani said, and Logan flicked her off.

"No. I'm talking about, what if there were a real place dedicated to pure bliss and orgasms? The sexiest men you could imagine just walking around and waiting to be picked out. Like a flower."

"I'd say you've been reading too many erotica books," Roze chimed in. "A place dedicated to doing nothing but getting your rocks off? Sounds too good to be true."

"But if it did exist, I'd be fucking everything walking!" Logan exclaimed, and we all laughed. "I'm so serious. I would be in heaven."

"Me too," Imani sighed. "Too bad a place like that doesn't exist. Now *that* would be the perfect getaway!"

"Yeah, too bad. . . ." I let my voice trail off.

They finished their breakfast talking among themselves. They hadn't even noticed that I'd withdrawn inside of myself. My thoughts were intrusive, but the main one that kept repeating over and over was that this was one of the last times I would get to have with them. My very best friends. Suddenly I didn't have much of an appetite. I pushed my plate away and excused myself to my bedroom. Once there, I shut the door behind me and sat down on my bed. I brought my hand to my mouth as I began to silently sob.

I planned a way to tell my friends about the cancer that had been eating away at my body. I'd never told them about it in the first place, all those years ago. And when I went into remission, I didn't see a point. I thought I had beaten it. It was supposed to be conquered and gone, but it came back. And when it did, I thought, *okay, no big deal. I can beat it again.* But I had been wrong. I was growing weaker by the day, and no treatment seemed to be working for me. Not even chemo. I'd been hoping for a miracle, but the reality of it all was that one wouldn't come. I had to face the inevitable.

That seemed so easy to do when I was at home alone, but in the faces of the people I loved, accepting that fate just seemed so selfish. Leaving them felt wrong. And in that moment as I cried my eyes out, guilt consumed me. I didn't want them to be mad at me or feel like I was giving up. I just wanted them to love me and love me hard. I wanted to spend as much time with them as I possibly could, and that meant going out there and facing them. Not only facing them but telling them the truth.

I took a deep breath and wiped the tears from my face. I would have to be strong if I was going to get through the day. My phone was on the nightstand beside the bed, and I grabbed it. Once I found the file I was looking for, I left the room.

"Ladies, could you please join me in the living room?" I called.

"Is there alcohol in there?" Logan called back.

"If you bring some!"

In the living room there was a large television on a glass stand. Connected to it was a cord that I could use to plug my phone in. When I did, I selected the slideshow I wanted to view, and by the time my friends arrived in the living room, the very first slide was frozen on the screen.

"'My Girls,'" Imani read on the TV and stared at the photo. "Aw, Dez, you made us a dedication video?"

I pressed play and sat down on one of the couches. She sat beside me, and the others sat on the other side of her. Imani's hands found mine, and she looked lovingly at me as the song "What About Your Friends" by TLC started to play.

"Oh, wow, is that from when we almost died in Madrid?" Roze gasped when a video of us zip-lining came across the screen.

I nodded and grinned. Madrid was the very first place we'd gone as the Travelistas and also the reason we had never gone zip-lining again. What was supposed to be a simple fun thing to do had almost turned deadly when we got stuck in the middle of the line. The helpers had to come rescue us.

"Aw, Dez, these are photos from when we went to Tulum!" Imani gushed as photos of us in front of her wedding venue slid onto the screen.

"We had so much fun even though Logan dislocated her arm," I said to her.

"Fuck Tulum!" Logan said and sipped the glass of wine she'd brought with her into the living room.

I laughed because I knew that would be her reaction when she saw the photos from that trip. But still, it was a part of our Travelistas memories. I made the slideshow, but I'd also watched it many times since we'd been there. Now I was watching their faces as they saw it for the first time. Some of the pictures and videos hadn't been seen in almost a decade. We'd changed so much. We'd grown into fierce women. And the slideshow of our time together was the best way for me to show my gratitude for our friendship. They weren't just my friends. They were my sisters. And there was no amount of time, distance, or space that would ever change that.

The end of the slideshow was filled with pictures and videos from our very first trip to Bali. And then it ended with our current trip to Bali, from our very first night partying, to us in our satin nightgowns, to us on the yacht yesterday. I felt a single tear fall from my eye when the last slide froze on the screen. It was the very first photo we'd ever taken together as a foursome back in college. The words on the screen said, Cheers to our last trip together. I love you. Always and forever.

"Umm, what does that mean? Last trip?" Imani asked with a furrowed brow.

"Yeah, because it's my turn to choose next, and y'all know I've been wanting to go to Turks and Caicos," Logan said and looked at me. "You trying to quit the Travelistas?"

"I'm not quitting by choice," I said and felt a knot forming in my throat.

Just say it. Tell them! I thought, but I couldn't. It was too hard. I couldn't face them. I should have just waited until I was back home in my house to even mention anything about it.

"Dez." Imani turned to face me, not letting my hands go. "What do you mean you're not quitting by choice? You know we're your girls, and you can tell us anything."

"I know. I just can't. I thought I could, but I can't."

"You can't tell us what?" Roze asked, getting up from the couch to kneel in front of me.

"It's bad, y'all. It's real bad."

I told myself I wouldn't cry, but that went down the drain. Tears rolled down my face. I hadn't even felt my eyes well up.

"What is it?" Logan asked, finishing her drink and setting it on the table. "You're acting like you're about to tell us you have cancer or something."

And just like that, my bomb was dropped. I took a big breath and looked at each of them with blurred vision. As the realization fell over them, I nodded my head to confirm any thought they had.

"Dez, I wasn't being serious. You have cancer?" Logan's eyes were wide.

"Yes," I told them. "I have cancer, and it's not looking too good for me."

"Okay, okay. We can beat this," Roze said, and Imani nodded. "We can beat this shit! There's all kinds of treatments, right? Right, Imani?"

"Yeah. People beat cancer all the time."

"I did beat it," I told them. "But it came back. I didn't tell you guys about the first time because I just didn't want to watch you grow tired of worrying about me. I didn't want to lose you."

"Never!" Imani said, wiping her tears away. "I would never leave you in a time of need. None of us would. You know this."

"And if you beat it before, you can do it again!"

"This time is different. The cancer is more aggressive, and it's not responding to any treatment. My doctor isn't sure I'll make it out this time."

"Well, fuck your doctor!" Logan exclaimed. "I'm not willing to accept what you're trying to say, so don't say it again!"

"Lo—"

"I don't want to hear it, Dez. I don't!" Logan put a shaky hand to her mouth as she began to sob.

Imani and Roze were next. I couldn't hold it in anymore either. I let my sorrowful sobs out. We held each other tightly and let the tears flow. My friends held on to me tightly, and I needed that more than they would ever know.

"I love you guys. I love you so much," I said, sniffling.

"And we love you too," Imani said, pulling away and grabbing her phone. "And that's why I'm changing our flights tomorrow. We're going home with you."

"No, no, you guys don't have to do that. I don't need Logan getting in trouble at work. And you guys have shit to handle with your husbands."

"Fuck that!" the three of them said in unison.

"You guys . . . I don't know what to say." I started to cry again.

I didn't know what I had done in life to deserve friends like them, but whatever it was, I was thankful I'd done it. After Imani changed everybody's flights, we stayed huddled together on that couch for the rest of the day, replaying the slideshow and talking about our favorite memories together. I loved them . . . my girls.

Part Two

Put the claws away, baby, because you know it's nothing like that. . . .

Chapter 14

Imani

I was awakened by the sound of someone bustling around my bedroom. I quickly opened my eyes and reached under my pillow, where I kept my pink .380. However, when I was able to focus my eyes, I saw that it was just Kevin. He was in the middle of zipping up the pants of his suit and slipping into his shoes. I let go of the gun to shield my eyes from the sunrays peeking through our window.

"Kevin, you know I hate when you open the blinds this early," I groaned.

"I'm sorry, baby. There's nothing like the views of a beautiful sunny day to get the day started."

"For you. Shut the blinds!" I said and threw my covers over my head.

I felt a dip in the bed when he sat down next to where I lay, and he pulled the cover back down. He gave me a look of pity that I hated. I just wanted him to leave so I could have the day to myself.

"Baby, are you going to get out of bed today?" he asked.

"Why does it matter to you? It's not like you'll be here."

"It matters to me because you've been moping around the house for months. Don't you think it's time to get out of bed? I thought you had those important red carpet dresses to design."

"Chante has them covered at the shop," I said, speaking of my assistant seamstress.

"Since when do you let someone else design your personal Imani Patrick pieces?" He raised his brow at me in a knowing manner. "Come on, baby. Dez wouldn't have wanted this for you. You have to let your life get back to normal sooner or later."

"My life being back to normal would include her in it," I said, biting back my tears. I turned my nose up at him. "Don't tell me how to mourn."

"It's been ten months, Imani. You haven't cooked or cleaned. Hell, you barely shower. Sometimes I think I married a zombie."

"Well, I'm sorry if me being sad about my best friend *dying* makes you uncomfortable. Actually, I'm not sorry, Kevin. And don't act like you care. You live such a fun life now. Coming home after ten o'clock smelling like cheap perfume."

"What? What are you talking about?"

"Whoever she is, I hope she makes you happy."

"Imani, you're talking crazy, so I'm about to just go to work and leave you here to sulk in peace."

"Yeah, and I bet you won't be home until midnight, huh?" I asked, half hoping he would say he'd be home early to be with me. However, the look of guilt on his face told me otherwise. "Just . . . just go, Kevin. Get the fuck out of my face."

He looked like he wanted to say something else, but if he did, I cut him short by throwing my blanket back over my head, shutting him out. I heard him get up and leave the room, and a few moments after that, I heard the chime of the alarm, letting me know he'd left through the garage. The second I was truly alone I did what I did every morning since Dez died. I cried. I cried my eyes out just like we'd done together our last day in Bali.

You would think someone who had quit her job and picked up to move to another state would be used to drastic changes. That I'd be able to adjust at the drop of a hat. But nothing in the world prepared me to lose one of my very best friends. Dez had been the glue between us all, and she was the strongest. So strong that I really believed that she would pull through and beat cancer.

After our trip to Bali, Roze, Logan, and I made good on our promise and stayed with Dez for an additional week. In that time, I was able to see all of the things she was hiding on vacation, like her pain medication and how tired she really was.

When we left her and went back to our own lives, her health really started to decline. But when her cancer progressed to stage IV, we had to prepare for the worst. And then the worst came. She died. I thought going to my best friend's funeral was going to be the hardest thing to bear. It wasn't. The hardest thing was living without her.

After she was gone, it started to hit me why she had been so spontaneous and unlike herself in Bali. She knew it was her last rodeo with her girls, so she went out with a bang. I was so grateful to her, and I would hold our last trip close to my heart forever. Never in a million years did I think that I'd have to say goodbye to Dez of all people. I planned to do what I had done most days recently: stay in bed all day and watch Lifetime. It made me feel like I wasn't crying at my own pain when I watched heart-wrenching movies.

I turned the television on and tried to get into the movie on the screen. However, my eyes kept drifting to my dresser. I tried to stay focused on the television, but when an adorable baby with a cute button nose came on the screen, I felt myself grow sick to my stomach. I quickly turned off the TV and threw the remote across the room with a cry of grief. My breathing was all over the place, and I tried to gather myself, but it seemed impossible at the moment.

I'd had dreams of having children with Kevin one day. Expanding our family was something I wanted to do once we were settled and successful in our careers. However, there we were, settled and successful, with no little ones running around. The thought of carrying the child of a cheater pained me. But not as much as the thought of a man only acting right for a child. If *I* alone wasn't enough for a man to get it together, then there wasn't a point in bearing his seed. Some might have thought it sounded crazy, but Dez would have understood. Feeling loved was how I thrived, and Kevin was doing a shit job of helping me thrive.

My feet seemed to move on their own, and I found myself out of bed and in front of my dresser. Slowly, I opened the top drawer and rummaged through some undergarments until my hand found what it was looking for. Pulling it out, I looked down at the old pregnancy test in my hand. My bottom lip quivered as I looked at the result, and I dropped it back in the drawer as if it were hot like fire. I slammed the drawer shut and got back in my bed. Throwing the covers back over me, I pinched my mouth shut to hold in my sob. I almost fell victim to another cry attack, but my phone ringing off the hook put a stop to that. I tried to ignore it, but whoever was trying to get in contact with me was relentless. Without looking, I reached under my pillow for my phone and answered it.

"Hello?" I said with an attitude.

"Damn, bitch. How many times do I have to call your ass to get you to answer the phone?" It was Logan.

"What do you want, Lo? I'm a little busy."

"Busy doing what? Lying in bed all day?" The way she said it was in more of a rhetorical manner, and I sat up.

"No. I'm actually sitting in bed, thank you very much."

"Yeah, whatever. Kevin called me and told me how you've been living. Come on, Mani, you have to get back to you."

"Since when do you talk to my husband on the phone?" I asked snottily.

"Put the claws away, baby, because you know it's nothing like that. He's worried about you. And frankly, after talking to him, so am I. Imani, we're all hurting right now. But that doesn't mean our lives stop."

"Do you hear yourself? We lost our best friend!"

"I know!" Logan shouted into the phone and took a deep breath. When she spoke again, her tone was softer. "I know. It hurts so bad. And every day there is a reminder on my social media accounts. Hell, all of the photos I have on my walls. I miss Dez like hell! Every day. But missing her isn't an excuse to give up."

"I'm not giving up."

"Like hell you're not. When's the last time you went outside?"

"Yesterday. To check the mail."

"Mani, be serious," she said, and I sighed.

"Fine. It's just hard moving on with my life. I just feel like it's so unfair that we still get to be here and she's gone. Like, she was so lively. And then she was just . . ."

"Dead."

"Yes. Sometimes I feel like I'm trapped in a nightmare. One I can't wake up from."

"We just have to make the best out of the days we have with each other and keep her memory alive. Speaking of which, you know what time it is, right?"

"Really, Logan? Really?"

"What? Dez would have wanted us to go."

"Dez should *be* here to go!"

"All I'm saying is it's time for us to meet and plan out our next Travelistas trip. We haven't broken the tradition in a decade, and Dez wouldn't want us to on her behalf. You know we meet every year for this now, Imani. Don't act brand new."

"Apparently I'm the only one in distress about it."

"You're not. It's just I have so much going on at work. I don't have the luxury of owning a business that works for me. And Roze is going through all of that crazy shit with Isaiah. So we need this, Imani. Plus—"

"Plus what?"

"Miss Debra wants us to come by to discuss Dez's estate."

"What?"

"She called last week. She wants us to come up this weekend."

I groaned at this new information. Mainly because she was right. I hadn't been answering the phone, and my voicemail inbox was full. I rubbed a hand over my face, feeling like I was being backed into a wall. I had to go. For Dez.

"All right. I'll go."

"Good. Because I really need you to book and pay for my flight."

"Yeah, yeah. Don't worry about it. I got you, girl."

"Thank you. So what do you think Miss Debra wants to talk to us about?"

"Knowing Dez? Only the Lord knows."

How could you do this to me? To our family? . . .

Chapter 15

Roze

"Liar!"

The clatter of glass breaking against the wall filled the air as I threw my fine china at Isaiah's head. To my dismay, he'd ducked right before the tea kettle could crash against his face. I could hear my daughters crying for me to stop, but I couldn't. I was on a mission, and it wouldn't be over until their father was lying in a pool of his own blood.

"Roze! Roze! Calm down! You're scaring the girls!" Isaiah shouted with his hands up, trying to protect himself from my wrath.

"Shut up, you cheating bastard!" I screamed, looking around the kitchen for something else to throw his way. "How could you do this to me? To our family?"

It was seven o'clock in the evening, and the day was ending in every way but peaceful. I'd finally connected all the dots to my husband's mysterious life. And all it took was me dropping lunch off to him at his office.

The ding of the elevator was loud as it let me off on the high-rise floor where my husband worked. Isaiah had surprised me with how supportive he'd been with me and the girls after Dez died. I didn't know if it had something to do with the fact that I was home more to grieve, or if he just truly cared about my emotions. Either way, he was on top of his husbandly duties. And I needed it, especially since life around me didn't pause when I wanted it to. I might have been at home more, but that was a job in itself. Isaiah had really stepped up, and I just wanted him to know how much I appreciated him. Pushed to the back of my mind were the hotel stays and weekends he was away.

I'd felt the ultimate loss when I lost Dez. I didn't have the capacity to lose anything else. Plus, I hadn't gotten any concrete proof that there was another woman, so I just decided to focus on making my family work. It also helped that we were making love again. In fact, that morning, Isaiah had his way with me in the kitchen right before he'd gone to work. I had to bite my lip and do Kegels when I flashed back to being bent over the stove.

My heels stabbed the floor as I walked, and everyone in the office smiled in my direction. They all knew who I was: Mrs. Henderson. The men knew not to stare too long, and the women admired my style. It was something I'd grown accustomed to, being a trophy wife and all. In my hands I carried a bag containing Isaiah's favorite loose meat sandwich from a restaurant he loved called Gretsky's. When I neared his office, I noticed that his secretary wasn't at her desk. She was a young blonde, fresh out of college, named Cassie. I didn't know much about her, but Isaiah said she did good at her job. Still, I would have to tell him about her disappearing act. It wasn't professional of her to leave her desk unattended like that. Anybody could walk into his office without a meeting. But me? I was his wife. I did what I wanted. I opened the door to his office and stepped inside.

"Baby, I know you're working, but I decided to bring your favori—"

I stopped midsentence in horror. It felt like I was in the most cliché episode of a soap opera, because I'd found Cassie. She was spread-eagled on my husband's desk as he rammed in and out of her with a handful of her breasts. All of the air in my lungs left me, and I couldn't speak. The worst part was that they were so indulged in each other that they hadn't even noticed they weren't alone anymore.

I wanted to rush up and start beating both of them, but my feet were glued in one spot. Isaiah was like an animal as he rammed in and out of Cassie, and from the twisted expression on her face, she was loving every second of it. My eyes fell to the blond bush between her legs, and I realized Isaiah wasn't even wearing a condom. I gasped loudly, and that time I was heard.

When Isaiah finally turned and saw me there, his expression quickly turned into a look of terror. He stepped away from Cassie and tried to come toward me, dick just flapping about. I dropped the food in my hands to the floor and made a beeline for the door. I was right. I knew it. He'd been having an affair the whole time!

The one thing I regretted about running out of Isaiah's office earlier was not giving him hell in the moment. But that was okay. The second he walked through the doors of our home, I unleashed all that hell on to him.

"I knew you were cheating on me!" I shouted and threw a butcher knife at him.

He ducked out of the way. I didn't know what hurt more, catching him cheating on me or the fact that he hadn't even bothered to strap up. I felt sick to my stomach as I remembered all of the love we'd been making as of late. I wanted to wash my mouth out and gargle with soap. "What did you expect me to do, Roze? You were too consumed by your career to worry about your husband's needs!" Isaiah shouted at me as he ducked out of the way of the fine china I hurled at him.

"What needs, you piece of shit?" I screeched. "We made vows! And just like you felt you weren't getting everything you wanted, I didn't either! But you didn't see me letting some random mother-fucker run up in me, did you?"

"Roze, please. I made a mistake."

"A mistake happens once. But this? How long has this been going on Isaiah, huh?"

"Roze . . ." He couldn't even look at me.

"That long, huh? Wow. And to add insult to in-jury, you cheat on me with a white woman?" I shouted. "A white woman, serious? You are just like these other trifling brothers running around here."

"Well, if you were doing everything you were supposed to, I wouldn't have had to go to Cassie for comfort."

"Oh, please! What you won't do is blame me for not being able to fight temptation. You're a dog, and I have something worse for you than fleas. Get out of my house, because the next knife I throw your way is going to hit its target!"

"You can't make me leave. This is my house too!"

"Not for long it's not. And when I'm through with you, you better hope you'll be able to afford some-thing as nice again. Get out!"

Isaiah didn't seem to like my threat. At all. In fact, he made a step toward me with an angry look on his face. But to my surprise our daughters ran toward me and stood between us. Maya hugged me tightly, and Aaliyah glared at him.

"You cheated on my mama with a white woman! I hate you! I hate you!" she shouted.

"And I hate you too!" Maya added. "Get out and leave my mama alone!"

The look of hurt on Isaiah's face brought satisfaction to my heart. It was proof right there that no matter how much time I spent inside of my career, my daughters knew how much I loved them. In that moment it was reciprocated times ten.

"Now you've turned my children against me."

"You've done that all by yourself," I said. "Now like I said already, get out. Your shit will be on the steps in the morning."

He sucked his teeth and nodded his head in defeat. He ran upstairs and grabbed a few things, but within minutes, he was gone. All of me wanted to break down and cry, but the way my daughters wrapped their arms around me, I knew I had all I needed right there. I hadn't meant for them to bear witness to all that they had. But that was the way it went down, and there was nothing I could do to change that. I kissed them both on the forehead.

"Help your mama clean up this mess."

"Okay," Maya replied.

Aaliyah went to pick up the butcher's knife and put it in the sink. She stared at it a few seconds and then back at me. My heart tugged when I saw tears in her eyes.

"I'm sorry, Mama. I should have told you."

"What?" I asked and rushed over to her. I lifted her chin gently so I could see her face. Her eyes carried a look of shame. "What is it, baby?"

"I . . . I saw them. Last year when you were with my TTs out of town. He was in your bedroom with Cassie. He thought Maya and I were asleep, but I wasn't. I saw him, Mama. I'm sorry!"

"He was in our bedroom with Cassie when I was in Bali?" I asked, and Aaliyah nodded. She burst into tears and buried her face in the stomach of my blouse. "Oh, baby, it's not your fault. I'm not mad at you. I'm sorry your father put you in that position."

I was really angry then. That son of a bitch wasn't just cheating on me. He was screwing her in my house, too? In my *bed?* Oh, yeah. I was going to take him for everything he had *and* what he didn't have. Bastard.

I consoled Aaliyah for a few more moments before I ushered both girls upstairs so I could just clean up by myself and order a pizza for dinner. I was in no mind to cook, and the kitchen was still a mess anyway. I was glad that my friends were coming into town that weekend. Lord knew I needed their support.

I was so confused, and my bottom lip quivered. . . .

Chapter 16

Logan

"Shit, shit, shit!"

I knew my neighbors underneath me weren't too happy about the way I was running back and forth in my apartment. My Uber would be there any minute, and I was trying to make sure I had everything I needed for my trip back home. When I was certain I was good, I rolled my suitcase out of the front door and ran smack dab into Nathan. Upon seeing him, I froze. Not out of fear, but out of pure shock.

"Well, it's nice to see you too," he said, noticing my not-so-friendly reaction to finding him there. "I've been calling and texting you."

"Did I answer?"

"No. That's why I decided to stop by today."

"Most people would take the hint and just move on," I said, locking up behind me.

"Going somewhere?" he asked, pointing at my suitcase.

"Yes, actually I am. I'm going to visit my friends."

"Oh, that's good. Especially after—"

"Yup," I cut him off. "We're going to plan our annual trip to get everything together."

We stood there awkwardly, taking in each other's images. He was still fine as ever, but his looks didn't move me. In fact, shortly after Dez passed away, I cut off all dead weight in my life, and that included Nathan. It wasn't just because he was bad in the bedroom. I just didn't want to be bothered. And it was clear that he would want to take things to the next step at one point. And I couldn't see myself tied down to a man who couldn't please me in the bedroom. Okay, maybe it did have something to do with him being bad in the bedroom. And in all fairness, I gave him many more chances after the Bali trip, and it just wasn't working out. It came down to the fact that, yes, he had most of the qualities I looked for in a partner, but the main one, the one that I couldn't compromise on, he didn't. And that made us incompatible. I'd let him down easy, but there he was still sniffing around.

"I miss you, Logan. I really do."

"Nath—"

"Wait, before you say anything, just hear me out. Whatever happened between us, I want to fix it. I know you were and probably are still going through a lot at the loss of your friend, but I feel like we can get through it together. I just . . . I just don't want to lose you."

I heard the sincerity in his voice. It was almost a plea. His expression was earnest, and he definitely would have been talking to my heart if it weren't for the icy layer covering it. I sighed in annoyance because all I wanted to do was go downstairs and catch my Uber. I shrugged and shook my head.

"Nathan, I think it would be best if you moved on with your life. And found someone who is willing to put up with your shortcomings. I have to go. I have a plane to catch."

Without bothering to excuse myself, I pushed passed him. I didn't need to look back to know his eyes were watching me as I walked away. I could feel them burning a hole in the back of my head. Hopefully he got the point that time. I would hate to have to change my number.

So much had changed since Dez had passed away. The old me had tried her hardest not to hurt Nathan's feelings, but the new me didn't care about that anymore. I wanted to put my energy in better places, not in tolerating a man who couldn't make me completely happy.

I didn't realize how much of a light Dez was on all of our lives until she wasn't there anymore to shed it. There were nights when I would go to call her to get her advice on something, but I would just end up crying my life away because I'd remember she couldn't pick up. She'd been the piece that connected our entire friend group, and as much as I hated to admit it, it was true. Roze, Imani, and I still talked, but it wasn't as often. I blamed it on the pain. And talking to each other seemed to make it worse sometimes.

Still, I was happy to finally be seeing them after so long. To be honest, I was completely okay with skipping our annual trip just like Imani until I got the call from Miss Debra about Dez's estate. I didn't even know she had an estate, and if she did, why hadn't it been presented closer to her funeral? Plus, the way Dez's ex-husband, Caleb, came around staking claim to everything, I was surprised there was anything left.

My Uber was parked right in front of my building, and the driver helped me put my suitcase in his trunk. Afterward, I got in the back of his Nissan Sentra and rested my head back when he pulled away from the curb. The ride to the airport from my house would be a little over a half hour, so I got comfortable. Right when my eyes closed, though, I felt my phone vibrate in my jeans pocket. I pulled it out, and when I saw who it said had texted me, my heart skipped a beat.

"Dez?" I said to myself and put my fingers to my mouth.

I was so confused, and my bottom lip quivered. Was it some sort of sick game someone was playing? I knew her parents had kept her phone active so that they could still hear her voice on her voicemail, but to my knowledge nobody actually used the phone. Taking a shaky breath, I slid the message open, and a small cry left my mouth when I saw a paragraph sent to me, Roze, and Imani.

My girls. My Travelistas. If you're reading this, that means I've crossed over. I know it's going to be hard, but just promise me you'll stay strong for each other. Reach out and love on each other more than ever before. I love you all so, so much. And I'm so excited about the journey you're about to embark on. Meet at my mother's house on our annual planning day at 7 p.m. She's expecting you. Oh, and Logan? Accept it. I won't take no for an answer. You'll know what I'm talking about.

I didn't realize tears were falling down my face until I was done reading the text message. I reacted to it with a heart, and shortly after, so did Roze and Imani. They'd seen it too. I took a big breath and let it out.

"Oh, Dez," I said, looking out of the car window. "What do you have up your sleeve?"

My family doesn't believe in divorce. . . .

Chapter 17

Roze

The days following the revelation of my husband's dirty deeds were filled with many emotions. The only time I felt completely at peace was when I was sleeping. However, that wasn't a permanent fix for my life completely going to shit. So when I was awake, I tried to keep myself as busy as possible with the house and the girls. I'd taken some personal days from my work. The last thing I wanted to see was happy couples buying their dream home together. I didn't need that kind of negativity in my life at the moment. Or was it positivity? Either way I didn't want to see it.

At first I found myself wandering down a road of blame in my mind. And it wasn't me blaming Isaiah. It was me blaming myself for everything being as screwed up as it was. Was it my fault that he'd found comfort in the arms of another woman? Had I really worked a number on him that bad that he would be with a white woman? Images of her being in my home, my *dream* home, sharing my bed with *my* husband, made me sick to my stomach.

However, I found my way back to common sense. I knew his actions weren't my fault. Isaiah was a grown man who knew how to make sound decisions. He could point the finger at me all he wanted, but the truth was the exact opposite of what he said. He wanted only what he wanted, and he didn't have a compromising bone in his body. I wished I could pinpoint when things got like that between us. Maybe we could have fixed them if they were caught early on. In the beginning we were a team, not a one-man show. However, we took vows, and he had broken them all. Instead of working on his marriage with his wife, he had chosen to step outside of it. And that was his cross to bear. And I was sure he had felt the complete weight of his actions when he was served with divorce papers on his desk. One thing I couldn't stand for any woman to deal with was a cheating-ass, lying-ass man. He could plead his case to the judge because I wasn't trying to hear it.

I hadn't told my girls about what had happened, although I had full intentions of doing so. If Dez were alive, she would have been the first one I called. In fact, I would have called her during all of the commotion. One thing about my sista was that she could keep a level head even in the most strenuous situations. I missed her like crazy, but I was happy when Friday finally rolled around and my other sistas would be in town. Since they would be staying with me, I woke up early to make sure everything was ready for them. I had two guest rooms, but I was sure we'd end up in one room especially since Isaiah's trifling behind wouldn't be there. I was in the middle of changing the bedding in one of the guest rooms when Nina came in. She rushed to take the sheets from my hands and shooed me away.

"Miss, I can do all of this. You go take a bath or something to relax! This is what you pay me for," she said to me.

"It's okay, Nina. I can do it." I tried to take the sheet back, but she pulled it out of my reach.

"No, miss. You have been going around this house doing my work these last few days when what you really need is to relax."

"I just want to keep myself busy."

"The girls told me all about Mr. Henderson, so you don't need to talk in circles with me," she said, giving me a knowing look. "You kicked him out, I'm guessing?"

"Yes. When he finds another place to stay, I will be mailing him all of his belongings. I filed for divorce."

"It's about time!" Nina exclaimed and went on to finish the job I'd started.

"And what's that supposed to mean? Did you know about his other woman, Nina?"

I stared at the elder Hispanic woman with wide eyes. If there was one person I trusted in my home it was Nina. Had she betrayed me too?

"I suspected there was something very wrong going on," she told me with a sigh. "There would be times where Mr. Henderson would give me clothes directly to wash instead of putting them in the hamper in your bedroom. Also, there were times he would send me home early, especially when you were out of town. I wouldn't even have the girls in bed yet. When I would come the next day, your bedroom would look like it had been ravished. I'm so sorry, Miss Roze, I should have said something sooner. But I—"

"Didn't have any solid proof."

"Yes," Nina said and stopped what she was doing to come over and place a gentle hand on my cheek. "A man like that doesn't deserve a rose like you. He should have been proud to have someone as hardworking and dedicated by his side. Most couldn't do that *and* be a good mother."

"I have you to thank for that," I told her, blinking away my tears. "If it weren't for all of the things you do around here, I wouldn't be able to be both a working woman and a mom."

"And I will always be here as long as you need me. Now go take a bath. Imani's flight gets here soon. I'm sure she got a rental so she could visit her mother while she's here, but if you hurry, I'm sure you can catch her at her favorite café."

"You think she'd be going to stop there today?"

"Doesn't she always?" Nina said with a wink.

She was right. Imani couldn't come home without going to her favorite spot. I nodded my head and made to leave the guest room. However, when I reached the doorway, I turned back to look at Nina. "Nina?"

"Yes, my dear?"

"Do you think I'm doing the right thing by filing for a divorce?" I asked, and her face softened.

"My family doesn't believe in divorce," she said, and I felt my shoulders get heavy. "But that's why none of the women in my family are happy. I love the men in my family, but they are the reason I never married. Listen to me, Roze: never ever let a man treat you like a doormat. And never stay in a situation where your smile fades and comes back as a fake one. You are young, vibrant, and have two young girls watching your every move. Find your strength and stay there."

I nodded again and left the room. Her words played over and over in my head all the way back to my bedroom. I also decided to take her advice and bathe before Imani's plane landed. I grabbed my phone to see exactly how much time I had, but my heart froze when I saw the screen. I had a text notification from Dez's phone, but how could that be? I swiped it open and read the group text. My hand went to my chest. Somehow, even from the grave, Dez always seemed to know when we needed some glue.

You were always too much for him. He had to go find less. . . .

Chapter 18

Imani

The moment I landed in Atlanta, I wanted to buy a plane ticket back home. I almost did, but I forced myself to be strong, which was easier said than done. The last time I'd stepped foot in that city was for Dez's funeral. The grief set in when I received a message from Dez's phone number. I'd just made it to my rental car and was about to hit the road when it came through in our group chat. Her words floated around in my mind as I read them in her voice. It was almost like she was sitting right next to me. She wanted us to meet at her mother's house later in the day.

Hurrying to tuck my phone away in my purse, I fell back into my seat. My eyes clenched shut as I tried to ward off my tears, but it was to no avail. They fell freely down my cheeks, and my bottom lip trembled. As much as I'd cried, I was surprised there was any water left in my eyes.

"Dez, you really fucked me up with this one," I said inside the Chevrolet Tahoe. "It's been so hard without you. But I'm going to get through this weekend for you."

I wiped my face, started the SUV, and drove out of the parking garage. As I cruised through the city, a nostalgic feeling came over me. I was home. Growing up in Atlanta made me the person I was today. Being surrounded by nothing but dreamers and doers, I had no choice but to constantly look to the sky. Making something of myself was inevitable.

Back in college, one of my favorite places to go was a family-owned coffee shop called the Wake Up Café in Buckhead. To me it was more than a place to get the best mochas. It was where I went to unwind and get myself together when I was stressing. It was my place of peace, which was why I always made time to go whenever I was back home. Logan and I had made plans with Roze to stay with her while we were in town, and I figured I had a little time to kill before Logan's plane landed.

The drive to the café was only about twenty-five minutes, and surprisingly traffic wasn't too bad that morning. When I arrived, I barely recognized the place on the outside or inside. The name was still the same, but the last time I'd come it was just a simple coffee shop with a counter to place your order and chairs to sit. Now everything had been upgraded to keep up with the times. The wooden tables had been replaced with glass, the simple light fixtures were now baby chandeliers, and there were even complimentary laptops against one of the walls for guests to use.

"What the . . . hell? This place has changed," I said to myself, looking around.

"First time here?" a voice asked, approaching me.

It belonged to a young, handsome man. He was tall, but even his beard couldn't hide his baby face. If I'd had to guess, I'd have said he was in his first or second year of college.

"It feels like it, especially looking around now. I come here whenever I come back to town, and just last year this place didn't have all the bells and whistles," I told him.

"Well, feel free to sit wherever you're comfortable. My name is Deon, and whenever you're ready to order, just do it from the tablet on your table, and I'll bring it out."

"Thank you."

I was choosing a table when the dinging of the door signified someone else had just entered. I didn't pay them any attention as I walked toward a booth in the far corner of the café. However, when I felt a hand grab my shoulder, I was forced to turn around.

"Hey, y—" I stopped midsentence when I saw Roze standing there.

"Something told me I'd find you here," she said and then put her hand on her hip.

"Roze, what are you doing here?"

"Looking for you obviously. I'm glad I came when I did since you never texted me and told me when your plane landed."

"Damn. My bad, girl. It slipped my mind. Honestly, being here, it's just . . ." My voice trailed off, and Roze gave me a sympathetic smile.

"Come on, let's sit down. We have some time to kill before Lo touches down."

We sat across from each other at the booth I'd chosen and looked over the menu, which was another thing that changed. A whole food menu had been added to it, and surprisingly it looked good. I felt my stomach growl, reminding me that I had barely eaten in days. It was right after 10:30, so I put an order in for a club sandwich and a side salad while Roze just ordered a cappuccino.

"Where are my nieces?" I asked once that was finished.

"At school. But they are spending time with their father at the hotel he's staying in this weekend," she said evenly.

"Oh, he's working this weekend?"

"Nope, he's living there until he can find an apartment. I filed for divorce."

My mouth fell open slightly. She'd just dropped the biggest bomb on me and spoken about it so casually. I studied her, and she seemed to be calm and collected, but I knew my friend. Roze didn't make rash decisions, especially not about something as life altering as a divorce. She wasn't telling me something.

"Are you sure that's what you want to do, Roze? I mean, you have the girls to think about."

"I am thinking about them," she snapped.

"By kicking their father out of the house?"

"Yes. They deserve a father who doesn't cheat on their mother. And I deserve a husband who is faithful to me."

"But you never even caught him doing anything," I said and watched a sadness come over her eyes. Her bottom lip trembled, and instinctively I reached out to grab her hand. "Wait, did you finally catch him?"

"Yes, I did." She nodded her head and blinked her tears away. "I walked in his office and caught that bastard on top of his secretary."

"Shut up! The white girl?" I exclaimed, and she nodded.

"I can't even tell you what I was thinking when I saw them. I was just numb. Numb at the fact that I was right, and scared because life as I've known it for so long is over."

"Oh, Roze. It's not over."

"It felt like it. All I could do was kick him out that same night. If I didn't, I was going to kill him. And that's not even the worst part, Imani. He had her in our bed. Our *bed!*"

"That son of a bitch!" I exclaimed. "I'm so sorry, honey. Nobody deserves this, especially you."

"It hurt so bad. So bad. All I ever tried to be was a good woman, and I *am* a good woman. Funny how that's not enough. I already am dealing with one loss, and now I'm maneuvering through another. Just pray for me, okay? Pray for my strength."

"You know I will. I guess the truth is that you were always too much for that man. He had to go find less, and it's his loss."

"Thanks." Roze sniffled and wiped her remaining tears away. "By the time I'm done with him, he won't have a pot to piss in."

When Deon came with our orders, I thanked him and dove right into my sandwich. The way I scarfed down the first couple bites, a person might have thought I'd been starved. My loss of appetite was due to my high stress levels. Prior, I simply had no interest in eating three times a day. Most times I just ate bowls of cereal. But that moment, my sandwich was so good I wished I had ordered two. Roze watched me eat with wide eyes.

"What?" I asked in between bites.

"I guess I've never seen you eat like a savage before," she said, sipping her drink. Her eyes never left me. In fact, they continued to watch me curiously. "You look thinner since the last time I saw you."

"I can't lose weight?"

"That's not what I'm saying."

"Then what *are* you saying?"

"Is . . . is everything okay, Imani? I'm worried about you."

For some reason her question irritated me. Of course everything wasn't okay. I still hadn't processed Dez's death, and my mourning process was draining me. I knew that, but I also didn't know how to heal myself. How does a person fix a heart they didn't break? And the only person who could make it whole again was the one person I'd never see again in the flesh.

"Am I the only one still mourning our friend's death?" I asked.

"Of course not! I can't believe you would even say something like that!"

"It just sure seems like it."

"Well, not all of us have a business that runs itself, Imani. Logan and I weren't able to put a complete pause on our lives, and I can't now especially. But don't ever in a million years think I don't miss Dez every day! You don't have that right."

A silence fell over us after that. She went back to sipping her cappuccino, and I finished my sandwich. I hated to admit it, but she was right. I didn't have the right to minimize her pain. We all had been dealt a great blow. Roze didn't deserve that.

Especially after coming to find me instead of waiting for me to show up at her house. Maybe she knew I needed her, or maybe she needed me. I reached out again and grabbed her hand. Our eyes connected, and before I could apologize, she nodded her head, forgiving me. She gave me a small smile and squeezed my hand.

"Tonight should be interesting, yeah?" she asked.

"I just hope Miss Debra isn't mad at me. I haven't reached out as much as I should have. I can't imagine what it's been like for her to lose her child."

"I could have made more calls too. But I'm sure she'll be happy to see us." Roze checked her watch and let my hand go. "I should get back to the house and get everything prepared for your stay."

"And I should head to the airport. Logan should be landing soon. After, we're going to visit our families, but when we get to your place, we can talk about this text message from Dez."

"That girl always had something up her sleeve." Roze shook her head. "I wonder what she meant when she said she's excited about the journey we're about to embark on."

"I don't know. But I'm sure we'll find out this evening."

When you know you're going to die, you have time to get all of your affairs in order. . . .

Chapter 19

Roze

It was 7:00 p.m. on the dot, and Imani, Logan, and I stood outside of Dez's family home. It was a beautiful Victorian-style house with a white picket fence surrounding the land. They'd taken a little longer visiting their families, so we were never able to sit down and have our own discussion about Dez's text. By the time they arrived at my house, they had just enough time to bring their luggage in before it was time to go. And finally, there we were, standing outside and staring at the house. None of us made the first move to ring the doorbell.

"Ring the doorbell, Lo," I said, nodding my head toward the door.

"Me? You're closest!"

"I just got my nails done. I can't." I knew how ridiculous it sounded once the words were out of my mouth.

"What?" Logan made a face at me.

"Fuck it. I'll be the brave one," Imani spoke up.

However, before she was able to press the bell, the front door swung wide open. Debra Vincent, Dez's mom, stood on the other side of it. A huge smile came across her face when she saw us.

"Oh, my goodness. It's so good to see you girls!" Miss Debra gushed when her eyes lay on us. "Come in, come in! Dinner is almost ready."

The three of us were still frozen where we stood. If I could guess, their reason was the same as mine. Dez had been the spitting image of her mother. They looked just alike. I felt my throat tightening as I stared into Miss Debra's face. But eventually I was able to force myself to smile and give her a hug before stepping inside of the house. Logan and Imani did the same thing, and we followed Miss Debra into the kitchen. On the way we were met with a plethora of memorabilia of Dez, mostly pictures, all along the walls. Her as a little girl, when she graduated college, and many photos of the four of us together. It made me happy to see that Dez's parents were keeping her spirit alive. For some, losing their daughter so early in life would have made it too painful to even look at her face.

"Here, sit at the table. I'll get you some wine," Miss Debra said and motioned to the dining room.

I noticed that five of the six places were set, and I wondered if Mr. Vincent would be joining us.

The three of us sat on one side of the table, and we watched Miss Debra bustle around the kitchen. She brought us glasses of wine before going to check the oven. When she deemed that her dish was finished, she took it out, and I was pleased to see that I was right.

"Mmm, I haven't had your lasagna in ages, Miss Debra," I said, sighing in delight.

"I wish you would come visit me more often. I'd make it for you whenever you like," Miss Debra said over her shoulder. "I haven't seen any of you girls since the funeral service."

I knew she didn't mean for it to be a blow, but it felt like it. What she said was true, though. I hadn't been over to see her since the funeral. I called and checked on her whenever I could, but I never seemed to find the time to stop by. Okay, okay. I had plenty of time to stop by, especially since I was the only one still living in the city, but it was just too hard. I'd only been inside for five minutes, and already all of the memories Dez and I had in the home were flooding back to me. Like when Dez and I snuck out of the house to go see boys, and when we snuck them in. Hell, I'd been there when I broke the news to Dez that I was expecting my first daughter. Right there at that very same kitchen table. I inhaled deeply at my sudden wave of emotions.

"I'm sorry, Miss Debra. It's just been so hard on all of us," I said with shame in my voice.

"You're telling me. I'm the one who lost a child," Miss Debra sighed as she loaded our plates with lasagna, breadsticks, and salad.

"I'm sorry. I didn't mean it like that," I apologized again quickly.

"I know, baby. Desiree was loved by so many people, especially you three. This hasn't been easy on any of us. But you have to keep living! No matter what, time stops for nobody. I just wish I had a little more time with my baby girl."

"We all do," Imani sadly chimed in. "I'm sorry, Miss Debra. I should have checked in more."

"Stop with the apologies. That's not what you girls are here for." Miss Debra brought our hot plates over to us and then sat down at the table. "There were some things we weren't able to get squared away as fast as we'd have liked to after Dez's death."

"Like what?" I asked, taking a bite of my lasagna. I didn't care that it just came out of the oven. It was staring me right in my face, looking scrumptious and cheesy. I had to have it. And the moment the flavor hit my tongue, I knew I was going to want a second piece even though my first was nowhere near gone.

"Before she passed, Dez appointed her father and me over her estate. I guess that's the only silver lining in all of this. When you know you're going to die, you have time to get all of your affairs in order. It's funny actually, how being very well prepared still never prepares you entirely. Monte and I buried Dez out of our own pockets."

"What?" I asked, shocked. "Now, Miss Debra, you know you could have asked me for whatever you needed!"

"It's okay." Miss Debra waved her hand like it was no big deal. "We are a very well-off family with all of the saving we do."

"But didn't Dez have life insurance? I thought she mentioned it in a conversation when she was filling out paperwork for her school," Logan said, and Miss Debra groaned.

"Ugh, that was such a mess. My baby did have life insurance, but it got wrapped up in a whole bunch of bull crap when that piece of dirt ex-husband of hers came sniffing around."

"Caleb? What did he do?"

"Well, for one, he never once called to check on her while she was sick. But once he found out about her five-hundred-thousand-dollar life insurance, he ran after it."

"Five hundred thousand dollars?" Logan asked with wide eyes.

Miss Debra nodded. "She got it years ago, before she was sick. I always asked her why so much money, and she would always tell me, 'You never know whose life a life could change.' That was my baby, always thinking about somebody else."

"Was Caleb her beneficiary?" I asked.

"He was at first, but then she changed it. He wasn't a happy camper when he found out about that. I can't stand that man! He didn't even come to the funeral, but he wanted to fight about some money! He tried to say that since she was so ill, she wasn't in her right state of mind when she took him off of the policy."

"Oh, that asshole!" Logan said and hit the table with her hand.

"Did they give him the money? He doesn't deserve a thing!" Imani shook her head.

"They almost did," Miss Debra told us. "It took a year, but finally they denied him. See, it was proven that Desiree had taken him off before they were divorced. At that time, she was in good health."

"Good!" I said with relief. "I'm glad you and Mr. Vincent were able to get that cleared away, even if it is a year later. You deserve that money!"

"Actually, we weren't the beneficiaries either," she said, looking at me.

"Then who—"

"So sorry I'm late!" a high-pitched voice interrupted me.

I turned my head and found myself looking at the most peculiar woman. And I mean that in a good way. In her hands was a big yellow envelope, but I paid it no mind. I was too busy staring at her features. She looked to be about our age and had hips for days with a small waist. Her skin was of a light complexion, and her long brown hair had loose curls that fell effortlessly around her shoulders. I didn't think I'd ever seen a black woman with freckles and green eyes before, but there she was in the flesh. She was very pretty and had the jaw structure of a model. I'd never met her before, but the way she hugged Miss Debra it was like they were old friends. I found myself wondering what was inside the envelope. She sat at the empty seat across from us.

"Oh, Mena, baby, it's okay. Are you hungry?"

"Starved," Mena said, holding her stomach. "And it smells like you made your famous lasagna, so you know I need a plate."

"Coming right up." Miss Debra got up and went to fix her food. When she came back, she set the plate down in front of Mena and sat next to her. "Girls, I'd like you to meet Mena. She was Desiree's lawyer and the one who oversaw all of my daughter's legalities. I invited her tonight so she could give you something."

"Give us what?" I asked.

"This," Mena said and opened the envelope she was holding.

From it she pulled three smaller white envelopes. I noticed that each had one of our names on it. Mena handed them to us, and I stared down at mine in confusion. The only way to clear that confusion was to see what was inside. I broke open the envelope, and from it I pulled a check. It was made out in the amount of a little over $166,000. Okay, opening the envelope hadn't helped. I was even more confused now. I looked up to see Miss Debra smiling at me.

"She named the three of you her beneficiaries, and I wouldn't have had it any other way," she told us. "As a mother it brings such joy to my heart to know you loved my daughter in all of the ways she could be loved. And that money is just a small fraction of the love she had for you, too."

"Miss Debra, wow. I don't know if I can accept this," Imani said, shaking her head.

"Yeah, what about you and Mr. Vincent?" Logan asked.

"Child, didn't you hear me say earlier that my husband and I are doing just fine? That's yours to have."

"Yes, she was pretty adamant about it," Mena chimed in and pulled something else out of the envelope. "And one more thing, Logan?"

"Yes?"

"Desiree wanted you to have these," Mena said and slid a set of car keys over to her. "And the car that goes with them."

"Her Mercedes?" Logan's eyes grew teary. "Oh, Dez. She loved that car."

"She loved you guys more," Mena said, offering us a kind smile and then turning to Miss Debra. "If you don't mind, I think I'm going to take my food to go. But before I do that, can I speak to the girls in private?"

"Of course, honey. You girls go on into the sitting room. I'll wrap all of your food up for you."

I didn't know what Mena needed to talk to us about out of earshot of Miss Debra, but I was curious. Roze, Logan, and I exchanged a glance as we followed Mena into the Vincent family sitting room. Mr. Vincent definitely had let his wife have her way in there. The furniture was all white, and a majority of the decor was made out of crystal, even the house phone sitting on top of one of the circular glass end tables. Mena sat down on one of the sofas, and the three of us sat on the other. I didn't know homegirl like that, so I for sure wasn't about to sit next to her. She seemed sweet, but still. After a few moments of us staring at each other, Mena cleared her throat.

"I guess the first thing I want to say is how sad I am that this is the way that we get to first meet each other," she said with an earnest look in her eyes. "Desiree always talked about you guys."

"I didn't think people usually met their friend's lawyers. I mean, unless they killed someone or

something," Logan blurted out, and I shot an in-
credulous look at her.

"Lo!"

"What? I'm just saying."

"Well, I was more than just Dez's lawyer," Mena
said and held out her hand, showing us a pink diamond ring. "I was her fiancée."

We started seeing each other last year. . . .

Chapter 20

Logan

It took everything I had not to fall out of my seat. Had I just heard that freakishly pretty woman right? Did she really just say that she was Dez's fiancée? But that would mean that Dez liked women, and that would make her a lesbian. Well, bisexual. It was a crazy thing to wrap my head around because, as far as I knew, I was the only one who'd dabbled on that side of things. Pussy was amazing, but I just liked dick so much more. And I thought Dez did too. I would have never guessed that she was into women.

I sat there staring at the beautiful heart-shaped diamond. My mouth was slightly open from the surprise of it all, but I hurried to shut it. I didn't know what to say. And from the silence, Imani and Roze didn't either. Slowly, we turned to look at each other. Their confused expressions matched how I felt inside.

"Well, say something," Mena said almost nervously and put her hand down.

Imani found her voice. "I mean, I don't know *what* to say."

"Right. I didn't know Dez was a lesbian," Roze said.

"Technically she didn't either until we fell in love," Mena said.

"How long were you two together?" I asked. "I can't imagine it being very long. We didn't even know she was seeing anybody."

"We started seeing each other last year."

"What?" the three of us said in unison. How had Dez hidden a whole relationship from us for that long? I didn't know how to feel. I thought we told each other everything. I guessed not.

"I respected her wishes to keep our relationship private. I understood what it was like exploring something new, but eventually she told her parents about us."

"Miss Debra knew too?" I asked.

"She did. They have always been so kind to me. They told me the only other time they'd seen their daughter that happy was when she was with you guys."

"Okay, so when did you two get engaged?" Imani asked, not even trying to hide the attitude in her voice.

"I asked her to marry me a month before she . . . before she died. But obviously we weren't able to."

I heard the sorrow in her voice, and my heart truly went out to her. She was grieving the loss of her lover. However, I didn't think my friends shared my sentiments. Roze leaned back and crossed her arms, while Imani shot daggers at the girl with her eyes.

"I don't believe it. Dez would have told us if she was engaged. She was our best friend!"

"And she was going to, but then she got so sick. Telling you guys about us was the last thing on her mind. I thought about coming up to you at the funeral, but it just didn't seem like the right time."

"Mm-hmm, I still don't believe it."

"You don't have to believe it, but we were in love. Dez was my soul mate, and your doubt won't take that away from me!" Mena snapped. She closed her eyes and took a deep breath to calm herself. Once she was okay, she unlocked her phone and handed it to us. "Here, look."

Since Roze was in the middle, she took the phone. It was open on a picture of Dez and Mena in Dez's bed together. They were certainly close. Roze swiped to another photo, and that one showed the two women kissing. She swiped some more, and we got a visual description of their love, all the way up to a photo of Mena curled up in

Dez's hospital bed with her. It was apparent that she'd loved Dez, and Imani had no right to challenge that.

"I'm sorry," Imani found it within herself to say. "I guess I'm not used to my friends not sharing important pieces of their lives with me."

"It's okay." Mena gave her a kind smile. "She told me that you all were firecrackers, so I expected some kind of uproar. I will say, I'm so glad that's out now. It's been a year, but it still doesn't feel real, you know? Especially since I'm still handling a lot of her business."

"It was you, wasn't it? You sent the text message," I said, suddenly connecting the dots.

"Text message?" Mena asked, confused. "What text message?"

"From Dez's phone," I elaborated, but she still looked confused.

"Dez probably figured out a way to future date her messages," Imani said. "You know these smartphones can do all kinds of things now."

While I was mulling that over, Mena reached inside the yellow envelope she had with her one more time and pulled out three plane tickets. She handed them to us, and when I looked at mine, I saw that it read a date a few months away. I was confused.

"What is this?"

"Dez knew it was Logan's turn to pick the next destination for the Travelistas," Mena started. "And I know this is the weekend you planned on discussing it. However, Dez wanted to give you one more parting gift: an all-expense-paid vacation to the location on those plane tickets."

"Saint Thomas," Roze read her ticket.

"Er, yeah. Something like that," Mena said.

"What do you mean something like that?" I asked, raising my eyebrow in her direction.

"You'll find out when you go. A few days before you depart, an email with an itinerary will be sent to you."

"I don't like the sound of that." Imani shook her head.

"Did you trust Dez?"

"Yes," we said in unison.

"Then trust her now in this moment. She really wanted you guys to visit the place we met."

"And where is that exactly?" I asked.

"Fantasy Island."

I'd never heard of a place called Fantasy Island, but it sounded like a place with lots of alcohol and food. Leave it to Dez to sneak in one last vacation even from the way beyond. I couldn't even be mad that she'd taken my turn. Plus, she'd gifted me a car that the Lord knew I needed. She'd also blessed me with the means to not only ship the car back to New York, but with the means to turn my life around. So if she wanted us to go to this Fantasy Island, so be it.

By that time, Miss Debra had finished packing our food and brought it to us. We stood up to go, thanking her for everything and giving her hugs. Mena stayed behind to talk some more with Miss Debra, but we left with our food and checks in tow. As we walked to Imani's rental, I could see the perplexed look on her face.

"What?" I asked from the back seat once we were all inside the SUV.

"I guess I'm still in shock, that's all." She shrugged. "A fiancée? Who's also a woman? I mean, damn, Dez, you could have prepared us for that shocker."

"That's what you're stuck on? I'm still pissed about Caleb's trifling ass. I can't believe he did all of that!" Roze said angrily.

"*And* didn't come to the funeral," I added, shaking my head. "I'm glad she found love in the end, though. I wish they could have gotten married. I'm sad for her."

"Me too. It feels like nobody around here is having luck finding happy endings," Roze said, and I reached to the passenger seat to pat her shoulder gently.

When I first arrived in Atlanta, I found out about Isaiah cheating on her. I was brokenhearted for my friend because I knew endings were always hard. But she deserved a man who would treat her the way she deserved to be treated. Isaiah was trash and deserved to be with trash.

"So about this trip, are we going?" Imani asked, driving off in the direction of Roze's place.

"I mean, do we have a choice?" Roze asked.

"Yes! And I'm going to be honest. I don't know about this. I've never even heard of a place called Fantasy Island, and I tried to Google it while we were inside."

"What did you find?" I asked, feeling silly that I hadn't thought to try to find the place on the internet.

"Nothing! The place doesn't exist."

"Well, we both know that sometimes places don't show up in the search when they're in foreign countries. It could be a hole-in-the-wall restaurant or something that Dez and Mena met at."

"I'm with Imani on this one, Lo," Roze said over her shoulder to me. "I love Dez, but I just don't know about this. I've never traveled blind before. We usually take time to research the places we're going to. This doesn't feel right."

"Our friend wouldn't send us anywhere that she felt was dangerous." I rolled my eyes at their skepticism.

"True," Imani sighed.

"So what do y'all say?" I asked, and the two of them looked at each other.

"We'll think about it," they said together.

You are wrong in every way. I need you to understand that. . . .

Chapter 21

Imani

Ironically, the trip to Atlanta, which I had questioned going on, seemed to be the thing I needed to put a pep back in my step. Knowing now that Dez had experienced love in her last days and had thought about us all the way until the end lessened the blow of her absence in a way. It reminded me that, even though she was gone, there would always be traces of her. She'd always be with us. I still didn't know about the Fantasy Island trip, but I'd be lying if I said I wasn't thinking about it.

When I got back home, the first thing I did was to go to my store. It had been a while since I showed my face there, but Monday morning it was the first place that saw me. I was dressed in my own line, wearing a cute yellow ruffled chiffon top with an above-the-knee skirt. My hair was freshly laid since my girls made me get a fresh install in Atlanta, and my makeup was flawless. I looked like a new woman, or should I say the old me. After parking, I walked toward my storefront and slowed my pace when I saw the fashion display in the window. It looked like something out of a horror movie. Well, not really, but it was all wrong. Nothing I would have done or approved. The spring catalogue was still being displayed, for one, and for two, I was almost positive more than one of the pieces were not my designs.

"What the fuck is going on?" I said to myself and stormed inside.

The sight that met my eyes made me want to gasp. As usual, there were customers inside of the store, but there was no one helping them. The rule was to be a companion shopper to all customers. We even had complimentary cheese and wine to offer them. However, each customer was alone, and no one was engaging with them. In fact, my employees were too busy laughing with and talking to each other.

"Do I pay you to entertain each other or to do your job?" my voice boomed.

Upon seeing me, my employees froze. My eyes surveyed them all until they landed on the person I was looking for. Chante Moses was my assistant seamstress and also the general manager of the store. Her shock in seeing me standing there quickly wore off, and she put a smile on her face.

"Imani! I didn't know you were coming in today!" she exclaimed in what sounded like a fake cheerful voice. She walked over to me in her pumps and held her arms out for a hug. However, I didn't have a hug to give.

I stepped back and pointed to the display in my window. "Obviously you didn't know I was coming in today, because that hideous representation of my brand wouldn't be there. My office, now."

I walked past her in the direction of the offices in the back. They were past the dressing rooms, so I had to put on a happy face as I passed the customers trying on clothes. I smiled, waved at and complimented them, but the moment we were in the employee-only area, the smile fell quickly from my face. I noticed that my office door was open, which was another no-no. And when I actually stepped inside, I was more furious.

"Whose shit is this on my desk?" I asked, pointing at a laptop and notebook that for sure weren't mine. I continued looking around the office and gasped. "And who the hell took my portraits down from the wall?"

My abstract portraits had been replaced with portraits of heels and dresses. Not original at all. And whoever had done it definitely didn't do so with me in mind. It wasn't just the photos. The positioning of my desk had changed, my comfy chair had been removed from the corner, *and* the sewing machine that had been gifted to me by my grand-mother was missing.

"Chante, you literally have two seconds to tell me what the hell is going on here," I said, looking at her with fire in my eyes.

"Okay, calm down," Chante said, putting her hands up. "You told me to take care of the store while you were taking your time off, and I made a few minor changes."

"Like taking over my office? What was wrong with your office?"

"I needed some help around here, so I hired an assistant. And she needed an office, so I gave her mine temporarily," she said.

"I wasn't informed about any new hires."

"I tried to call and let you know, but your hus-band told me that you trust me to take care of your business. He told me to make any changes I felt necessary."

"Oh, he did, did he? And did those changes mean adding your own unapproved designs to my cata-logue?"

"I, well, I—"

"And not only that, you put them in the dis-play, using my likeness on something I don't even like," I said incredulously. "I'm trying my hardest to keep a level head, but I asked you to take care of my business, *not* take advantage of me in a time of loss. This is the Imani Patrick line, not the

Chante Moses line. I don't know who you think you are—"

"I'm the one who did your job when you couldn't," she spat.

It surprised me honestly. But it was just the boost I needed to really cut loose.

"No, you're the employee who is doing the job you're paid to do. My husband has no ownership of my business, so listening to him was your first mistake. Your second mistake was putting someone on my payroll who I don't know and have never met. She could be a spy for another company for all I know." I turned up my nose at her like she was the most disgusting thing I'd ever laid eyes on. "And your last mistake was not going based on the design notebook, which specifically details the pieces that are to be produced. None of that cheap shit you have in my *fucking* window!"

Chante jumped back in her heels. I was sure my voice had carried to the front of the store, but I didn't care. My breathing was hard, and my anger wasn't subsiding anytime soon. *How dare they?* I knew I had fault in it as well, but was I so wrong to think that the people I trusted would handle things correctly? Let me rephrase that: thought I trusted. My business was the one thing that I could say was mine and all mine. I couldn't believe that Chante would be as sneaky as the snake in the garden.

"I'm sorry, Imani. I just really wanted people to see my designs. I love creating your ideas, but I just . . . I don't know. I was so stupid, and I'm so sorry!"

Chante hung her head down. She was younger than me, about the same age I was when I first started taking designing seriously. I knew she was hungry, but to do what she had done was career ruining. I wanted to fire her with every fiber in my being. No, I wanted to slap the hell out of her and *then* fire her. But as I watched her literally shaking in her shoes, I remembered something. I remembered how it felt to have a dream and how I would have done anything to reach it. I took a deep breath and released as much negative energy as I could.

"I want the new girl fired expeditiously. You need your old office back."

"Ma'am?" she stammered. "I'm not fired?"

"No," I sighed. "As angry as I am right now, I do still appreciate you for keeping the doors open here on my downtime. You are wrong in every way. I need you to understand that."

"I do."

"And those designs are hideous, which is why you'll need time to perfect your solo craft. I'm going to allow you to design a fall dress line under Imani Patrick. I, of course, will have to add my touch in the end, but you can name it whatever you want. If I like it—no, if I love it—it can be a part of my end-of-summer fashion show, and you will receive designer credit."

"The Imani Patrick fashion show?" Chante's eyes grew big. "I know I've helped design things for it before, but oh, my God. This is huge for me. But why?"

"I hired you because I see myself in you, and I still do. Now get your shit out of my office and clear that display! I want the correct summer line front and center," I said, turning on my heels. "I'll be back later. I have a husband to curse out."

You selfish bitch! . . .

Chapter 22

Imani

I couldn't get out of the store and back inside of my car any faster. I sped the entire way home, not even thinking about what I was going to say to Kevin. He had the nerve to act so concerned when he was the main reason my business would have gone to shit. Who was he to tell someone to do whatever they wanted with *my* business? I couldn't believe him. I felt my anger boiling over again, and when I pulled into the driveway, I'd barely put the car in park before I hopped out.

"Kevin!" I shouted when I barged through the front door. The click-clack of my heels echoed throughout the house as I ran around in search of him. "Kevin!"

"Whoa, whoa, what's the commotion about? I'm right here." Kevin emerged from the kitchen wearing a suit, and he had a sandwich in his hand. "Wow, baby, you look great! You finally got out of bed I see. You headed to the store?"

"I just left it, actually," I said, tossing my purse and keys to the side. Next I kicked off my shoes.

"Did something happen?"

"Why do you think something happened, dear husband?"

"Because you're kicking your shoes off like you're about to fight somebody."

"Kevin, don't play with me right now. I'm trying my hardest to not knock that fucking sandwich out of your hands." I looked at the ceiling and clapped my hands together as if that would calm me down. "Please tell me why you told Chante she could do whatever she wanted with my store."

"She's the general manager," he said and shrugged. "That's her job."

"If she called *me* to discuss anything, why would *you* take it upon yourself to make a decision? That's *my* business."

"A business you wouldn't have been able to open if it weren't for me."

"Let me tell you something," I said, walking up to him and putting my finger in his face. "Don't ever do that again. My business is the one paying all the bills around here, even *with* me being as down and out as I was. I checked my bank statements. Where the hell is all of your money going?"

"I'm not doing this right now. I'm late from lunch." Kevin took a bite of his sandwich and tried to head for the door.

"No, we're doing this *right* now!" I shouted and grabbed his arm to stop him. "You piece of shit, who is she? Huh? Who's the bitch taking all of your money?"

"I'm not cheating on you!"

"You're lying! Where else is all of your money going?" I asked and started frantically digging in his suit pockets.

"Imani, wh . . . Stop! What are you doing?" He tried to stop me, but eventually I found his cell phone.

Kevin had never been as secretive with his phone as he was before Dez died. And after, I was in such a funk that I just stopped caring about the mystery phone calls. I wasted no time right then in going through it.

"I wasn't able to catch you last year when I put cameras in the house. But I saw you going out all dressed up. Who were you going to see? Your side bitch?"

"You put cameras in the house to spy on me?" he asked, horrified.

"Sure did, when I went to Bali. But you were too smart to bring her to the house, huh?" I shook my head. I continued to scroll through the phone until my eyes stopped on a name that seemed to come up frequently in his call and text log. "Who's Nadia?"

"Imani, I can explain. Just give me my phone back."

"No," I said and opened the thread to read the messages. My heart dropped at what I saw. "'The deposit went through.' 'Thank you for the flowers.' 'Looking forward to seeing you tonight.' Oh, my God. Kevin, I knew it!"

I threw the phone at him and clutched my chest. I felt like I couldn't breathe. I'd seen more than what I read out loud, and it was very apparent that he had been spending a lot of time with Nadia over the past year. I couldn't believe it.

"Imani . . ." Kevin tried to step toward me, but I slapped him hard across the face.

"After all I've done for you, this is how you repay me?" I said, allowing the tears to fall from my eyes. "It all makes sense. Why you barely fuck me, why you suddenly don't have any money . . . I can't believe I didn't see it."

"It's not what you think."

"Yeah, it's not what I think. It's what I saw. You're a liar. But you know what? Maybe I deserve it because I've been keeping a secret from you too," I said. The inner me was screaming to not say it. I could feel her trying to hold me back, but my angry side was more powerful.

"A secret? What secret?"

"I was pregnant."

"Pregnant? When? What?"

"I was pregnant, and I aborted our baby!" I said and watched how my words stung him far worse than my slap did.

"Imani . . . what?" His eyes were huge. "Why would you do something like that?"

"When I got back from Bali is when I found out. I didn't want to have the child of a man who was cheating on me."

"You know I've always wanted kids, Imani. With my low sperm count, I thought I couldn't have kids. And you killed it? How could you do something like this to me?"

"Fuck you, you piece of shit! I'm glad I did. I wouldn't want anyone to turn out like you. I hate you! Maybe you can have Nadia give you a child."

Tears fell down his face, and seeing him in pain made me feel good. I felt like I was holding his beating heart in my hand. He deserved it, every ounce of it. I'd done my due diligence as a wife, and what did I get back? A lying, cheating husband. I smirked and turned around to leave him to pick his own jaw up off the floor. However, before I could take one step to the stairs, I felt a set of strong arms lift me up in the air and slam me down. He turned me to face him, and suddenly it didn't feel like I was in the presence of my husband. He was deranged.

"Kevin!" I shouted and tried to wiggle away, but his grip on me was airtight. "Let me go!"

"You selfish bitch!" he bellowed in my face through his sobs. "How could you do this? How? I never cheated on you!"

"Then who's Nadia?"

"She's my business account manager! I made the decision last year to go into business for myself. You inspired me so much by having a successful business, I wanted to know what it was like to be my own boss."

"Then why are you depositing money in her account?"

"I never deposited money in her account! That deposit went into my business account. And I sent her flowers when she helped close a deal on the location I wanted. She's happily married with children, something I don't think I'll ever have with you. All of this was supposed to be a surprise. I was working sunup to sundown trying to get all of this together. I was too tired to fuck you every day! We're married, for crying out loud! A marriage is based on more than sex."

"Kevin, I—"

"Shut the fuck up! All of this was supposed to be a surprise. I thought you trusted me, but you don't. And you killed my baby in the process. I don't think I can come back from this. I can't even stand to look at you. We're done."

"Wait. Kevin!"

I was so filled with shame that my body shook. I'd never seen him so worked up, and he'd never laid a hand on me. I kept trying to get my hands on him to pull him back, but he just kept pushing me away. There were no words to say to ease his pain, a pain that just minutes ago I was happy to have brought him. Now I would do anything to take it back.

Eventually I fell to the ground and wrapped my arms around his legs, crying and begging him to stay. Snot fell out of my nose, and my eyes were too blurry to see. I didn't want him to leave. He kicked me off of him, and I fell to the ground. He looked down at me pitifully.

"I'll be back to get my shit. Don't call me."

And with that, he slammed the door.

I knew I liked you. You have a spine. . . .

Chapter 23

Logan

Something about the trip to Atlanta had me on a cloud. Maybe it was the fact that I got to see my family and spend time with my girls. Or maybe it was because I had come home with some dollars in my pocket. After depositing the money in the bank, the thought of quitting my job definitely crossed my mind. But I didn't.

It was a lot of money, $166,000, but it wasn't $1 million. And that meant it wasn't enough to live off of if I wanted to make it big with my art. So instead, I came up with a plan to use it to fund my first big art showcase. I would invite anybody who was anybody in New York. If I did it all the right way, it could be the break I needed. In fact, I was in the middle of planning and research when Bethany burst into my office with a thick folder in her hands. I hurried to shut my laptop and act like I had been doing something productive.

Ever since my promotion, I'd been able to see my boss in a brighter light. She was good at her job, but I figured out a part of that was because she didn't have any friends. Not to mention, all of her family had moved from New York, so she was all alone. It made her the perfect machine to run a company. She didn't have anybody to hold her back. It was a little sad, actually. But it helped me to give her more grace when she did things like barge in my office without knocking.

"Can I help you, Bethany?" I asked in a pleasant tone.

"Yes, you sure can. I need you to run these claim numbers through the system and make sure they were done correctly." Bethany dropped the folder in front of me.

"So these are completed claims?" I asked, confused, thumbing through the papers.

"Yes, they are, but while you were on vacation, a few people got lazy. One of our clients almost received a hefty payout when their claim should have been denied," she told me.

There was an implied undertone there. Like if I had been there instead of out of town, then it wouldn't have happened. I almost rolled my eyes. I enjoyed the promotion, and the pay raise was amazing, but I didn't like being responsible for the performance of the entire work floor. Moments like that were making walking out and never looking back seem more worthwhile. But instead, I smiled and nodded.

"Of course I'll take a look at them."

"Good. I'd like them back by the end of the day. And also, would you mind rescheduling my one o'clock and replacing them with my noon appointment?"

The hairs on the back of my neck stood up. Nowhere in my job description did it say that I would be doing my work plus the work of a secretary. *Hold it in. Don't say anything.* But of course, that was too much like right.

"Yes, I do."

"Excuse me?"

"I said, yes, I do mind," I told her with a smile on my face. "You have a secretary, and I'm sure she'll be more than happy to move your appointments around. I, however, have work to do, and now that you have added more work to my load, I won't have any time for anything else today."

When I was finished speaking, a glare came over Bethany's blue eyes. She didn't blink for a while the whole time she stared at me, and I held her gaze. Maybe it was in my head, but I swore a chill had suddenly come across the room. Finally, Bethany's stony expression softened.

"I knew I liked you. You have a spine, kid."

That was all she said before she left my office, closing the door behind her. When she was gone, I realized I was holding my breath. I let it out in one big exhale. I couldn't believe I had just done that. For a moment I was sure the T-Rex was going to bite my head off. But then again, I had read somewhere that women don't get anywhere in life without being assertive. Had I just earned her respect? I was smiling inwardly at myself and preparing to hop on my workload when I heard a vibrating sound. Remembering I'd put my phone on vibrate, I fished through my tote bag in search of it.

"Hello?" I answered once I found it.

"Good, you answered the phone." Roze's relieved voice came through the other end. "Imani is on the other end having a crisis."

"What's wron—"

"Hold on. I'm about to merge you," she said and clicked over. After a second, she clicked back over. "Hello? Is everybody here?"

"I'm here," I said.

"I'm herrre!" Imani's voice wailed.

It was followed by a long bout of her sobbing and saying things I didn't understand. My girl was stressed out. I knew we'd just had our annual Atlanta meetup, and I was thinking maybe it had all been too much on her. She seemed to be okay while we were there, but grief struck everybody differently.

"Mani, slow down. I can't understand a word you're saying," I said into the phone.

"Ke . . . Kevin left me!" Imani was able to get out.

"Kevin did *what?*"

"He left her, girl," Roze chimed in. "She accused him of cheating, and he wasn't!"

"Imani, you didn't," I groaned.

"I did. I found messages in his phone, and I was wrong the whole time! And that's not the worst paaart!"

"Go ahead and tell her," Roze said. "Tell her what you told me."

"I told him that I got an abortion. I threw it in his face to hurt him when I thought I had him cornered. And he left me. He *left* me!"

"Oh, my God," was all I could muster.

It was all so much to wrap my head around. First, Isaiah cheated on Roze and now she was getting a divorce. Then it was finding out about Dez's lesbian relationship to now finding out that Imani got an abortion. I never even knew she was pregnant.

"Say something, Lo!" Imani cried.

"I don't know what to say. I just . . . is it true? That you got an abortion? Are you telling the truth?"

"Yes. I didn't tell anyone. It was something I did by myself, and I was going to take it to the grave. But I weaponized it. I wanted to hurt him so bad, and I just ended up ruining my marriage."

"When the fuck were you pregnant?" Roze asked. "There were no signs."

"Wait," I said, racking my mind. I thought back to the last trip where we were all together. "Bali. You kept throwing up."

"Yup. I was pregnant. Only four weeks. I didn't find out until I got back," Imani said sadly. "I didn't want to have a child with a man who wasn't faithful. And I was wrong the whole time. Now I just feel shame. I killed my baby."

"Well, at that point it was just a parasite anyway," Roze told her.

"Roze!" I exclaimed.

"What? Y'all know I had an abortion in college when Rodney's trifling ass kept nutting in me. I was not about to have his baby, and that's what my mama told me to get me through it. It worked. I don't even think about it anymore."

"Well, this is different!" Imani wailed again. "Kevin has a low sperm count. They told us we might not ever have kids of our own. And now that he knows I took away what could be his only chance to have a baby, he hates me."

"Oh, Imani, no, he doesn't," I said, trying to ease her pain.

"*He hates me.*" Her shout was so loud that I had to pull the phone away from my ear for a moment. "My marriage is over. My life is over. I don't know what I'm going to do."

The phone line grew quiet of words. The only thing I could hear was them breathing. Roze was at a point where she was desensitized, and well, I had never experienced a bond that deep. I felt that everything I wanted to say would sound generic, and I didn't want to upset Imani more than what she already was.

I was disappointed in her. Not because she had gotten an abortion, but because she hadn't told us a word. *Us*—her best friends and ride or dies for life. I couldn't imagine the burden it must have been to hold on to a secret like that for all that time. Secrets like that were like a ticking time bomb. When they finally came out, it would always be like an explosion went off. In Imani's case, her marriage was in ruins.

Lost in thought, I began rummaging through my desk. I stopped when my eyes fell on a small envelope. It was the one Mena had given to us containing our checks. I had forgotten that I'd tucked it away in my drawer after I'd gone to the bank that morning. Pulling it out, I dumped the remaining contents on my desk. The set of car keys were there. I still had to get the Mercedes shipped to New York once the check cleared. That wasn't what I was focused on, though. I was too busy staring at the plane ticket.

"Fantasy Island," I finally said, breaking the silence.

"What?" Roze asked.

"Fantasy Island. Let's go. Dez wanted us to."

"I'm not thinking about a vacation right now. My marriage is in the toilet!"

"Mine too," Roze agreed. "I don't think now is the right time to do our trip. Maybe we should wait until next year."

"Don't you see? Now is the perfect time to go!" I told them, feeling myself getting worked up. "Roze, you need a breath of fresh air after the ringer Isaiah has put you through. Right? And, Imani, you need a reminder of who the fuck you are. And me? I just need another trip with my best friends."

"Lo, I don't know. . . ." Roze's voice trailed off.

"Are we really going to disrespect Dez's memory by not honoring her last wishes of us? We haven't missed an annual trip since we started the Travelistas. I say we go and have the best time of our lives. I'm sure it's not called Fantasy Island for no reason, right?"

They were silent, but I knew they knew I was right. There was a reason why Dez wanted us to go to whatever and wherever Fantasy Island was. And I trusted Dez. Not only that, but we needed the trip. There had been so much sadness looming in the air for the past year, it was time for a change. And if we couldn't find our way back to happiness at first, peace was a great first stop.

"What do you guys say?" I asked after they still hadn't said anything.

"Imani, it's your call," Roze said.

"Fuck it." Imani sniffled. "I'd rather be with my girls than alone in this big-ass house, drowning in the sorrow of my fucked-up decisions."

"Good. Then it's settled. Fantasy Island, here we come!"

Part Three

The Past

I was celebrating life, and in order to do that, I had to live to the fullest of my capability. . . .

Chapter 24

Dez

"Okay, makeup bag, toiletries, flat iron. Check, check, and check!" I said as I checked the list on my phone.

My suitcase was packed, and I was ready to head to the airport. I'd gotten a fresh sew-in the day before, and I was feeling myself to say the least. However, even though I lived alone, I felt like I was sneaking out of the house. Not only that, but I felt like I was cheating. And I knew why. My best friends and I normally took our big vacations together, and there I was about to go overseas without them. It wasn't anything I was doing maliciously, however. I was celebrating something that they knew nothing about. Being in remission for a year was a big deal to me. Not only because I felt that I'd beaten a ferocious disease, but because I'd fought it by myself. My parents didn't even know about the cancer that had been eating away at my body.

Me not telling them had everything to do with not wanting to give in to defeat. If I had let any of them know, my phone would have never stopped ringing and I would have been constantly reminded that I was sick. I had never been one to have people worrying over me. For as long as I could remember, I was the rock in all of my relationships. And I made the decision to be my own rock. I thought that was what helped me heal, but still, I was always cautious because I knew there was a chance that the cancer could come back. Every day was a gift.

I'd decided to drive myself to the airport and park there until I returned home. My friends and family would be under the impression that I was away at a summer teacher's retreat somewhere in Denver. Really, I would be on the beautiful beaches of Saint Thomas, enjoying myself. I finished zipping up my luggage and headed toward the door. I was a few hours early for my flight, but after checking my bags and getting through TSA, I would probably only have half an hour to read the book I was bringing along. As I was reaching for the doorknob, my phone began to ring from inside of my fanny pack.

"Hello?" I answered after pulling it out.

"Dez, I need you! It's an emergency!" Roze cried on the other end of the phone.

"What? What happened?"

"Maya's ass swallowed a penny! I can't *believe* this girl, but I'm freaking out. What should I do?"

"Is she acting fine?" I asked.

"Yes, for now. But it happened only about twenty minutes ago. Has this happened to any of your students?"

"Well, my students are too old to do anything like swallow a penny," I told her, stifling my chuckle. "But the penny should pass just fine through her stool. If you're truly concerned, take her by the emergency room."

"Okay. Thanks, girl. I think I'll do that. Do you think you can come with?"

"I wish I could, but my flight leaves in a few."

"Oh, shoot. That's today? I completely spaced. Well, I can hold the fort down. You just have a good time on your teacher's retreat! Hopefully it won't be too boring."

"Oh, I'm sure I'll be able to find something entertaining to do. Love you!"

"I love you too!"

When she hung up the phone, I went to put the device back inside of my fanny pack, but it started to ring again in my hand. I thought it was Roze again, but it wasn't. It was Logan. I watched it ring for a few moments, contemplating if I should just let it go to voicemail. Of course I didn't.

"Hello?"

"Hey. I'm sorry to call so early," Logan said. That was usually what she started with when she knew she was about to ask for something.

"What do you want, Lo?"

"Oh, nothing, just to not be homeless. I'm a little short on rent this month. My paintings didn't sell as well as I thought they would on that online store I told you about last month. I just need five hundred. Please?"

"Lo, you know I love you and always have your back, but you really have to start budgeting your money better."

That was what I said because it sounded like the responsible thing to say. But the truth was I personally budgeted $1,000 a month to help Logan with her monthly expenses. See, she didn't come from a well-off family like I did. Her mom helped when she could, but Logan was all the way in New York by herself, living her dream of becoming a world-renowned artist. It was something I always admired about her. Not many would take that leap of faith with no support, but she did. And contrary to her needing help here and there, Logan was doing pretty well for herself. Plus, I was never one to judge a person's happiness with a dollar sign.

"I did budget this month, but that all went to food! You know I'm a bigger girl. I need to eat. Shit!" she exclaimed, and I laughed.

"I will wire it once I get to the airport," I told her, and she sighed in relief.

"Thanks. You are a lifesaver."

"Don't mention it."

"Okay, I won't! Call me when you get to Denver!"

"I'll send you a text here and there. They have us doing all kinds of activities, so I might be too busy to call." The lies just seeped through my teeth.

"That's fine. As long as I hear from you. Safe travels, sista! I love you."

"I love you too!"

That time when I hung up the phone, I stood there, staring at it. I didn't know what it was about my friends, but it was like they had some kind of telepathy going on. When one called, the others followed. And with two out of the way, that left one to go. And sure enough, barely after a minute had passed, my phone rang again. Imani's contact info popped up on the caller ID, and I clicked the green answer button.

"Hey, girl," I said, wondering what it was she needed.

"Hey, baby! I was just trying to catch you before your flight to tell you I hope you have a safe trip and I love you!"

"Well, aren't you sweet?" I said, smiling and feeling slightly guilty at my previous assumption.

"Just a little bit. Are you all packed?"

"Yup. I'm on my way out the door now. I just got off the phone with Roze and Lo."

"Ugh, those heffas are always beating me to the punch. Whatever, just make sure you text me when you get there! You know those white folks get to acting crazy out of town sometimes!"

"I will be sure to let you all know that I didn't get kidnapped by an angry white mob."

"That's all I ask! But I just got to the store. I'll talk to you later!"

"All right. Love you!"

When we were off the phone, I was finally able to make it out of the house and to my car. After loading my luggage in the trunk, I started my journey to the airport. I didn't know why I felt so anxious. It wasn't my first trip alone, but this time it felt different. I didn't know what to expect, but I was open to whatever came my way as long as it didn't involve doing drugs of any kind or being in the wrong place at the wrong time. I was celebrating life, and in order to do that, I had to live to the fullest of my capability. Whatever was in store for me, I just hoped that it was ready for me. Or me for it.

Gone was Prince Charming only to be replaced with Lord Farquaad. . . .

Chapter 25

Dez

The first thing that hit me when I stepped off of the plane was the warmth of the sun. It was enough to change my mind about taking a nap first thing once I got to the Rio Spa Resort. I couldn't fathom wasting such a beautiful day. So instead of going to sleep when I checked into my large suite, I took a shower and put on a pretty orange dress. It hugged me in all the right places and stopped just above the knees.

There were a few restaurants attached to the resort, and I chose the one right off the beach. It had a wraparound bar, but I opted to sit at one of the tables. It was midday, and the sound of the waves crashing into land was soothing. After ordering a Long Island iced tea, I sat back and enjoyed the beautiful view. When the server brought back my drink, I placed an order for a club sandwich. The last thing I wanted was to have a hunger headache my first day of vacation.

After taking my order, the young woman left, and I went back to scoping out the scene. There were many people along the beach, but my eyes fell on a couple in the distance. They were young and had golden brown skin. The woman's smile said it all—there wasn't anywhere else she'd rather be than with her man in that moment.

Watching them love on each other made me think back to my ex-husband. Caleb West had been, at one point, the man of my dreams. I'd met him right after college, and he presented himself as the perfect gentleman. Tall, dark, and handsome. Just how I liked them. I used to daydream about what our chocolate babies would look like. I almost laughed as I sipped my drink. I really wanted to pop out that man's babies. Wow, God definitely helped me dodge a major bullet with that one.

See, Caleb was the perfect example of being a wolf in sheep's clothing. Shortly after we got married, gone was the sheep, and out came the wolf. When we first had gotten together, he was attentive. He held doors, never stayed out too late, and couldn't keep his hands off of me. Hook and bait. But once he knew he had me? Gone was Prince Charming only to be replaced with Lord Farquaad. He stopped holding doors and coming home on time, and he barely wanted to touch me.

"If I don't want to sleep with you, who else would? You're black as hell and ugly."

That was just one of his coined phrases. I couldn't say when the verbal abuse started, but when it did, it never stopped. The funny thing was that he must have forgotten my parents had spoken life into me since I was in the womb. His words didn't hurt, but the fact that he was *trying* to hurt me did. His biggest mistake was thinking that I wasn't going to leave him. And once I found out about him stealing from his clients, it gave me the perfect out. I declined the alimony. I wanted ties severed completely with that man.

That was the story I told anyone who asked me about my ex-husband. I could paint a better picture, but what a waste of time that would be. My girls also knew better than to bring him up. He wasn't worth the breath. Having cancer had shown me all too well how short life was, and I didn't like spending it on dealing with or talking about things that didn't bring me joy.

My food came out rather quickly, but I wasn't complaining. Hell, how long did it take to make a sandwich? I dived into it and relished the first bite. Delicious. I barely had swallowed the first when I took a second. I felt my body do a little dance. Food was definitely the way to my heart.

"That good, huh?" a voice asked.

"What?" I glanced up to see a tanned Caucasian man standing near my table.

He didn't look to be much older than me and had a muscular build. His eyes were brown and matched the hair on his head. He was wearing a T-shirt that hugged his biceps and a pair of floral shorts. The smile he was flashing at me was blinding, and his teeth were perfect. I didn't dabble with the white meat, but he was a good-looking man, I had to admit.

"The sandwich," he said and pointed at the porcelain plate in front of me. "I couldn't help but notice your happy dance as I passed."

"Oh, that. It's nothing. Just a girl enjoying her meal."

I was trying to be polite, but I could tell by the way he was looking at me that he had hopes of continuing a conversation. I wasn't really in the mood to use my voice. I just wanted to enjoy being still for a moment. Maybe take a walk on the beach when I was finished with my drink. I was hoping the gentleman got the picture, but of course he didn't. In fact, he had the nerve to sit down in the chair across from me at the table. I was, to say the least, shocked.

"Umm . . ."

"I'm sorry, I just have to be straightforward with you. My eyes have been on you since you walked over here. I had to come and say something. Maybe have something to eat with you." He turned and waved the waitress back over to the table. "My name is Jay, by the way."

"Well, Jay, it's nice to meet you, but umm . . ." I cleared my throat, trying to keep my agitation at bay.

"It's nice to meet you too . . ." He lingered on the last word, and I knew he was waiting for me to tell him my name.

"Marie," I lied.

He was a nice-looking man, but I didn't know him. And the Girl Code handbook said to always give a fake name if unsure. I didn't care how charming he seemed. He was getting on my nerves, and I wanted him to move.

"What brings you to Saint Thomas, Marie?" he asked, and I just stared at him for a while without saying anything. "Did you not hear my question? What brings you here?"

"Not to be rude, Jay, but since you have no problem with it, I'll just come right out and say it. Most people don't like it when people invite themselves to their table."

"Well, you aren't most people. A woman doesn't travel alone and dress as beautifully as you if she doesn't want some sort of attention, am I right?"

I scoffed. I honestly wanted to pinch myself because I couldn't believe that was happening to me. Not only that, but he was serious. I felt completely disrespected that he would violate my space like that. It was the most entitled thing a person could do. Not to mention, he hadn't even asked for my name. He just knew he liked what he saw.

"Actually"—he held a finger up to me when the server approached the table again—"I'd like to order a steak, medium, with a side of—"

"Umm, excuse me?" I couldn't take another moment of that obnoxious man. That was not how I wanted to start my vacation off. "I actually *do* mind you sitting here. I never said it was okay for you to join me. I don't know you, nor do I want to get to know you."

"Would you two like me to come back?" the server asked nervously as she looked back and forth from Jay to me.

"No, you can serve him over there somewhere," I said and pointed at one of the tables far away from me. "But he needs to go."

"It's all right. I know when I'm not wanted," Jay said, holding his hands up. "I'll have my steak over there."

"Yeah, you do that," I said, rolling my eyes when he got up and left.

"Are you okay, miss?" the server asked, and I nodded.

"I'm fine. It's just the nerve of some people."

She smiled and nodded before following Jay and taking his order. I went back to enjoying my food. Or trying to, anyway. I attempted to focus back on the happy people on the beach, except there was a burning sensation on my cheek. Well, that was what it felt like when you could tell somebody was looking at you. I turned my head, and sure enough, there was Jay seated at a corner table across the restaurant with his eyes glued on me. He no longer had a smile in his eyes. He was glaring at me. I thought he would look away after he knew I could see his hateful gaze, but he didn't. If anything, the glare grew more intense.

An uneasy feeling came over me, and I decided that it was time to leave. I paid for my food and drink before hurrying to get up from the table. Jay's eyes followed me all the way around the bar and back into the resort. I power walked through the many people inside until I reached an elevator. Before I got on it, I glanced over my shoulder to make sure I wasn't followed. When I saw that the coast was clear, I got on and pressed the number to my floor. *Next time grab your Mace.*

I couldn't help but wonder how he knew I'd traveled alone. Just because I was eating by myself didn't mean I hadn't come with someone. Maybe he was just fishing for information. I quickly shook the thought from my head when the elevator let me off on my floor.

I walked toward my room at the end of the empty hall. I could hear music coming from one of the rooms and laughter coming from many. It suddenly dawned on me that I hadn't checked in with my friends yet to tell them I made it here safely. I pulled out my phone and typed out a message in our group chat. With my focus on my phone, I didn't even notice that the elevator had dinged behind me again and that someone had gotten off on my floor. I finally reached my room and was about to open the door with my key when suddenly I felt warm breathing on my neck.

"What a rude *bitch* you are. I think somebody should teach you a lesson!" a man's gruff voice said.

A strong hand grabbed my arm and forced me to turn around to face him. It was Jay. He must have been following me. My feet suddenly felt glued to the floor, and I was stuck. I couldn't move. I didn't know if it was shock, fear, or a mixture of both. But staring into his crazy eyes, I knew nothing good was about to come from the altercation.

It was then that I remembered all of my father's cautions about women traveling alone. There were crazy people in the world. And they only got crazier when they didn't get what they wanted. In that case, I didn't know what Jay wanted, but I could take a good guess. His eyes traveled down to my cleavage and back up to my face.

"You know, when I first saw you get off the plane, I thought, *I could make a lot of money off a pretty thing like her.*"

His words sent chills down my spine. He'd watched me get off the plane. That meant he had followed me to the resort and was just waiting for his chance. He'd targeted me. He placed his palms on the door behind me, blocking me in.

"Didn't anybody ever tell you how dangerous it is to travel alone?" he taunted me. "Now I want to do this the easy way. You come with me down the stairs in the back, no funny business. You can run, but there are four men just like me in the lobby prepared for that to happen. You won't get far. There is no escaping me."

The girls and I often joked about sex traffickers, but to be face-to-face with one made me want to throw up the few bites of sandwich that were in my stomach. He was going to kidnap me, and I was never going to see my family again. The thought was one I couldn't accept, not while I still had breath in me.

"Well, I can try!" I said right before kneeing him as hard as I could in the nuts.

It was enough to double him over momentarily. I took the chance and ran as fast as I could to the elevator. It felt like in seconds he was right on my tail. I tried to scream, but he grabbed me up in the air and threw me down to the ground, knocking the wind out of me. In the distance there was another elevator ding, but the only thing I could focus on was Jay pulling out zip ties and a hand-kerchief from his pocket. I tried to scream again, but by then he'd forced the handkerchief on my face, covering my mouth and nose. I didn't mean to inhale, but I did, and in seconds I felt myself go lightheaded. The last thing I remembered seeing was a flash and Jay being knocked off of me. Then I was out.

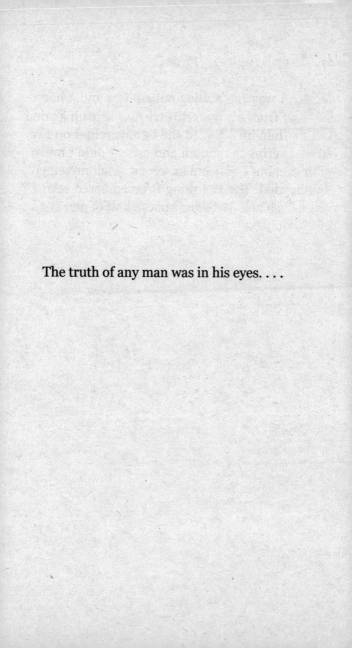

The truth of any man was in his eyes. . . .

Chapter 26

Dez

"Mmmm!"

My mouth naturally released a groan as I woke up from what seemed like the longest slumber of my life. Last I remembered, the sun was still shining, but now the moon was high in the sky. I could see it from where I lay on the bed. *Wait.* I hurried to sit up and look around at my surroundings. *Bad idea.*

"Owww!" I said, touching the back of my head.

My body had a dull ache going on, too. Slowly everything was coming back to me, from the creepy guy at the restaurant to him following me to my room. He had tried to kidnap me, but there I was in my bedroom suite surrounded just as I'd left it. My suitcase was open and in the corner. The bathroom counter was a mess from when I did a quick face beat. *But how?*

"You should lie back down. You hit your head pretty hard when he threw you."

The voice came from a chair in the corner. A man was sitting and watching me with a look of concern on his face. He had olive skin and a freshly trimmed beard. Not knowing who he was or if he was with Jay, I looked around for something to protect myself with. The only thing near me was the telephone, so I picked up the receiver and held it in a defensive manner.

"Stay the hell away from me! I'm calling the police!"

"Miss, I assure you I'm not here to hurt you," he said, holding his hands up.

"Oh, yeah? And how am I supposed to know that? For all I know, your friend is waiting outside the door to snatch me up!"

"Friend?" He made a disgusted face. "I would never run around with a scumbag like him. What men like him do is wrong."

"And who are you?"

"I am Alejandro."

"Okay, Alejandro. Where do you fit in all of this?"

"I first saw him at the airport earlier today. I couldn't help but notice his eyes go to all the young women. Most were traveling in pairs or groups, but you weren't. When I saw him start to follow you out of the airport, I knew something wasn't right."

"And what were *you* doing at the airport? Trying to pick up women too?"

"Yes," he said, and when I made a face, he waved his hands. "No, not like that. I am a driver. I take people from the hotel to a special resort. However, the guests I was waiting for never showed up. I was about to go back, but then I saw what was about to happen. I cannot stop it from happening all the time, but I knew I would wonder what happened to you for the rest of my life if I didn't do something."

"So you followed him following me?"

"Precisely."

"You were at the restaurant too?"

"Yes. At the bar. These guys' usual game is to charm their way into the lives of their victims. But you did not make that easy for him." Alejandro chuckled a bit. "You pissed him off. I was afraid that I was not going to make it in time. I didn't know what floor you'd gone to, so I pressed all of them. But I finally found you and saw him on top of you. I hit him in the head with a fire extinguisher, and he ran off."

"I think I remember seeing that," I said softly.

I looked at the receiver in my hand and then back at Alejandro. I didn't know him either, but something else my father had always taught me was that the truth of any man was in his eyes. And looking in Alejandro's eyes, I found peace. There was no threat there. Still, I was apprehensive as I put the phone back on the hook.

"What is your name, miss?" he asked.

"It's . . . Desiree," I told him. "I guess I should thank you. If it weren't for you, I guess I'd be in the back of somebody's van getting drugged up and addicted to cocaine."

"Don't thank me yet," Alejandro said and shook his head. "It isn't safe for you here. The person who tried to do this may come back to finish what he started."

He was right. Just because Jay, if that really was his name, had been stopped once, it didn't mean he wouldn't try again. Suddenly I began to panic. I wasn't safe. How had I been so naive to not pay attention to the fact that I was being followed? So much for a beautiful vacation. I was going where it was safe: home.

"I'm about to look up flights to go back home," I said and got up in search of my phone.

I couldn't find it at first and felt my anxiety spike. What if Jay took it? My mind began playing all kinds of horrible scenarios. However, a sigh of relief came when I found it on the other side of the bed on the floor. I started looking up flights immediately.

"I hate that this is your experience here. You shouldn't have to leave so soon," Alejandro said.

"If I'm not safe, then I don't know any other option."

"What if I had another alternative? Where you can stay and enjoy your time here?".

"If it doesn't involve me getting gangbanged by a group of fat fucks, I'm all ears." I briefly placed my phone in my lap but didn't close out of the flight option screen.

"I told you before that the guests we were expecting didn't show up."

"What does that have to do with me?" I asked with a shoulder shrug to urge him to get to the point.

"Their entire stay is paid for and has a no-refund clause. I'm sure under the circumstances I can pull some strings and get everything switched over for you."

"But can't that guy and the people he's connected with find me there too?" I asked, and Alejandro gave a mysterious smirk.

"Where you will be going, they won't be able to get to. All I need is for you to say yes, and we can leave."

"Wait." I shook my head and tried to wrap my mind around what was happening. "What is this place?"

"It's a place that is invite only. Because it's the place where your deepest and even your darkest longings can come true. You choose your own path, but I can guarantee that when the stay is done, you'll have found a new you . . . inside of you."

"What the fuck does that mean, Alejandro? You're speaking in riddles and shit!"

"Just say yes, Desiree."

"Fine," I exclaimed. "Yes!"

I was more lost than the dogs in *Homeward Bound*. . . .

Chapter 27

Dez

Now some might have called me a fool for leaving with a man I didn't know after another man I didn't know tried to sex traffic me. And although I didn't completely trust Alejandro, he *had* saved my life and that had to count for something. He also was trying to save my vacation, and I couldn't lie, the resort he had spoken so mysteriously about had really gotten my attention.

He helped me put my luggage and bags in his Jeep and we left the Rio Spa Resort. As we drove, I could feel the soft rumble of the engine under my legs. The night was still young, so the island was alive with people. Many different scents hit my nostrils as we passed different food spots and nightclubs. If I had been there with my girls, we would have tried to hit as many places as we could. Alejandro played his music and sang along with all the songs. I almost laughed at how into them he was.

We drove for a while, and I almost got nervous when we got to a part of the island that was so far from everything else. What if him saving me had just been a ruse to throw me off? That thought left my head the moment I saw us approaching what had to have been the resort in the distance. It was a little ways off the beach and was bigger than the one I'd just left. Right in front there was a huge fountain made up of mermaids with crystal clear water spouting out of their tails. In big, bright letters on the building was the word WONDERLAND, and I figured that was the name of the resort. Alejandro drove around and parked in front of the entrance, where a bellhop wearing a red uniform greeted us.

"Alejandro! We were expecting you hours ago. Is everything okay?" the bellhop asked.

"Everything is fine, David. Will you wait out here with our guest while I speak with the front desk?" Alejandro asked him.

There was a curious look on David's face, but he didn't deny Alejandro's request. His eyes fell on my luggage and then on me when we were alone. He looked to be in his early twenties, and I could tell by his features that he was an islander.

"You must be going around to the other entrance," David said and winked at me.

"Umm, other entrance?" I asked, wrinkling my brow.

"Yes, see, some guests pay to stay here, but a lot go to the *other* place," he said, winking again.

I felt like he thought I knew what he was talking about. But really I was more lost than the dogs in *Homeward Bound*. I made a confused face and prepared to ask him what the hell he was talking about, but by then Alejandro had returned.

"All right, perfect. We got you all set. You will just need to check in on the other side."

"You mean the other entrance?"

"Yes. I see David must have told you all about it." Alejandro smiled and shook David's hand. "I'll be back after I get Miss Desiree settled."

He got back in the Jeep and drove us to the far side of the well-lit building. I sat up a little bit in my seat to see exactly where he was taking me. He made a quick right, and we were face-to-face with a golden brass gate. It was tall and looked like something out of *Game of Thrones*. There was a low humming sound when the gate opened, and Alejandro drove us through.

"What the . . ." I heard the words come out of my mouth.

"The bosses are working on an entrance directly through the resort, but for now we still go through the gate," Alejandro explained as he drove.

"An entrance to where?"

"Where you'll be staying." He smiled and then pointed. I followed his finger, and my eyes widened. "Where we were was the main resort for our regular guests. However, this building here is only for the invited."

In front of me was a resort behind the one we'd just come from. It was smaller and not able to be seen from the front, but still big. Alejandro pointed to the back of the first resort and drew an air line to the front of the second.

"Soon they will be connected there, and it will be easier for guests to get in and out. Come. I will park and help you to your room."

He pulled to the front, and that time there was no bellhop to greet us. Alejandro helped me with my luggage and led me to the entrance. He walked through the automatic sliding doors, but I hesitated.

"Alejandro?"

"Yes, Miss Desiree?"

"How do I know I can trust you?" I asked even though I knew it was something I should have asked before agreeing to go with him. "How do I know when I walk in there I won't be murdered or something?"

Alejandro's eyes softened at my hesitance. He set my bags down briefly and approached me. He took my hands in his and sighed before he started talking.

"Miss Desiree, I would never put you in harm's way. I would not have intercepted today if I wanted to hurt you. If you do not mind my bluntness, you are a beautiful woman who has traveled this far by yourself."

"I'm celebrating," I told him, but for some reason when I said it that time, I didn't even believe it myself.

"Do you have friends?"

"Yes."

"Then why are you here alone? You are either running from something or hiding. It might not be either of those things. But it is something. And when you walk through these doors, I can promise you that you'll find it and heal it. So to answer your question, yes. You can trust me."

I had no words. I took a big breath and nodded my head. He gave me an encouraging smile and let my hands go. I followed him inside of the cold building. The moment I was all the way through, I felt a rush of relief come over me. Although it was nighttime, there were many people walking around, and they all had smiles on their faces. The sound of their voices and laughter did my soul good after the day I had. Not only that, but there were other black people! And only black people knew how good it felt to see other brothas and sistas in the mix. To the far right of me there was a bar where guests were mingling and having a good time. Seeing the relief on my face, Alejandro laughed and led me to the left where the front desk was. Waiting was a young island woman who had a big smile on her face as she stared at me. Something told me she was expecting me.

"Miss Desiree, this is Leah. I think she can take it from here," Alejandro said and held his hand out.

After I shook it and said my goodbyes, he set my luggage down again and was gone. I turned back to a smiling Leah and pulled out my ID and handed it to her. I knew the drill when it came to checking in.

"Thank you, Miss"—she checked my ID— "Vincent! It looks like for the next three days you'll be staying in the Sunset Suite. Great choice. The name I'm sure is self-explanatory. You get the best view of the sunset from your balcony."

"Wait, three days?" I said, making sure I'd heard her correctly. "I'm here for a week."

"Oh, I'm sorry. The attendant of the other front desk told me you would need an explanation. No worries. When Madam Freya comes by your room, she'll explain everything. The elevators are just down this hall, and you're on the fifth floor."

After typing some things in her computer, Leah handed me my ID along with a key card. I didn't know what else to do except gather my things and head for the elevator. So far nothing about the first day of my vacation had gone according to plan. But then again, what had *been* my plan? Maybe I needed a little bit of spontaneity in my life. Well, minus the almost getting kidnapped part. Definitely could have gone without that. But if Alejandro had dropped me off at some sort of cult, it was going to take all of Saint Thomas to get my foot out of his ass.

Your sexual energy will always reveal who you truly are. . . .

Chapter 28

Dez

Okay, first things first. My suite? Amazing. It was so spacious, and the bedroom was separated from the living room. The appliances were all stainless steel and looked like they hadn't ever been used. The marble floor had golden specks in it that matched the golden fans on the ceiling. It was basically a luxury apartment. I wouldn't be able to see the sunset view Leah was talking about until the next evening, but for right then the ocean view would do just fine. The moon reflected off the water, and I couldn't help but stand there and stare. If I had it my way, I'd stay on the balcony for the rest of the night, but a knock on the door prevented that.

I stepped back inside and went to look through the peephole. On the other side of the door was a different island woman wearing white scrubs and toting a cart. She was short and wore her hair in a messy bun. On her face was a pleasant expression, but I was wondering what she wanted. Surely it was too late for housekeeping. Cautiously I opened the door a crack and peeked out.

"Can I help you?" I asked.

"Hey, Desiree, I'm Madam Freya. Leah told me that you knew I'd be stopping by."

I did remember Leah mentioning her name, and that was the reason I eventually stepped back and let her in the room. She pulled her cart inside with her and stationed it in the living room. I glanced at what was on the cart and was befuddled to be looking at the same kind of tools my ob-gyn used when she did my STD testing.

"Do you mind if we sit down for a moment?" she asked.

"As long as you tell me what all that is for." I pointed at the cart.

"Of course," she said, and we sat down across from each other on the couches. "So first I want to apologize for coming so late. Normally we're able to get the exams over much earlier so that results come back as soon as possible. But with you being a surprise guest and all, exceptions were made."

"Exam?" I made a face, and she laughed.

"Nothing crazy. We take a sample of your urine and do a finger prick. Also a rapid HIV test."

"You're testing me for STDs?" I asked, feeling myself panic again. "Oh, my God. Oh, my God. I *am* being sex trafficked."

"Desiree, calm down," Madam Freya said and cautioned me to take a deep breath. "I am here to test you for STDs, but it isn't for what you think. Here, take a look at something else I brought you."

From the bottom of the cart, she grabbed a pamphlet and handed it to me. I took it, curious to see what it was. The first thing that popped out to me was the sexy naked couple on the front. They were entangled on top of silk sheets and staring lovingly at each other. The second thing that stood out to me were the words "Fantasy Island." When I opened it, I realized that it was a brochure showcasing what were called fantasy packages.

"'The Mandingo package,'" I read out loud. "'The Lover's Lane package'? 'Euphoria'? 'Build Your Own'? Build my own what?"

I looked back up at Madam Freya, and she had the same mysterious look in her eyes that Alejandro had earlier. I looked back down at the brochure and read the descriptions of the packages, and my jaw almost hit the floor.

"What you have in your hands is the way you get to build your own fantasy for a week. Whatever you want, we have. Whatever you need, we have."

"So it's a sex camp."

"No. It's Fantasy Island. The place where your dreams come true."

"My sexual dreams?"

"Yes," Madam Freya answered simply. "But it's deeper than that. Your sexual energy will always reveal who you truly are. There is no judgment on Fantasy Island. Everybody desires something different. However, we draw the line with minors and persons who are disabled or criminally insane. We do have midgets, though, if that's your thing. You also will have the choice of adding other guests to your packages."

"So everyone I saw downstairs in the bar. They're—"

"Waiting for their results to come back to go to the island."

"Hold on," I sighed and held my hands up. "*This* isn't Fantasy Island?"

"No, silly." Madam Freya laughed loudly. "This is the intake resort. We are huge on safety in every shape and form. We test all of our guests, so as long as everything comes back negative, you'll be welcome on the island and able to enjoy pure bliss. I know all of this sounds crazy, and this is the reason why it's invite only. And only chosen guests are able to bring in new guests. Usually they know what they're getting into before they come."

"Okay."

It was all I could think of to say. It didn't sound real, but something in me was telling me it was. Madam Freya didn't look like a crazy person, and neither did Alejandro or Leah. My eyes fell on the cart and lingered for a moment before I took out my phone. Madam Freya gave me a disappointed look.

"If this is not something you want, then—"

"No," I cut her off. "I mean, yeah. It's just, what if I already have recent results? Like within the last week recent? Blood work and all."

Being that I was in remission, I still constantly got my blood drawn by my doctor. I also got tested for STDs every three months. I was divorced, not a nun. And because I was still sexually active, I liked to stay on top of my sexual health. Coincidentally, I had gone to the doctor right before my trip, and my results had been uploaded on MyChart. I was able to log into it and hand it to Madam Freya. She looked over it attentively, scrolling with her thumb. When she was done, she handed the phone back to me.

"Those test results are recent enough to suffice. But that's one part of the screening process."

"Okay, what's next?"

"Just a small questionnaire," Madam Freya said and pulled a small notepad from her pocket.

"Umm, okay. Fire away, I guess."

"Great, first question. When is the last time you were heartbroken?"

"Umm, what? Why do you need to know that?" I raised my nose. I didn't know why she needed to be that far into my business.

"Miss Vincent, I know you might not trust anything going on around you, but I'm going to ask you to try. Please answer the question."

Her face was soft, but her eyes stared intently at me. I could feel the answer to her question rising up out of me. Very much like when Ursula took Ariel's voice. Except Madam Freya didn't give me evil vibes. She was . . . safe. I took a deep breath and blew it out up my face.

"Fine. This is something nobody knows, not even my friends. They see me as this strong Amazon who can't break. Well, I broke. It was after my divorce."

"Tell me about it."

"Let's just say the phrase 'things change' hit me like a box of bricks with Caleb."

"Caleb being your ex-husband?" Madam Freya asked as she jotted something down in her notepad.

"That's him. Slimy bastard. I thought we would be together forever. When we first met, it was rainbows and butterflies. Hell, fireworks if you will. But after a while, he showed me who he truly was. A monster."

"He hit you?"

"He might as well have, but his words got the job done," I told her. "He tried his hardest to make me feel worthless. Unwanted. He tried to make me hate my appearance. But that didn't work."

"And is that what broke your heart?"

"The words? No. But the fact that he said them brought me to the end of the plank." I looked down at my French pedicure and felt a sadness welling up inside. "It broke my heart that somebody who I loved so much could *try* to make me feel lower than dirt. And it broke my heart to think about the aftermath of it if he'd succeeded. What kind of woman would I have become? And would that have been better than being the other option? A failure?"

"You think you're a failure?"

"I'm the one all of my friends come to when any little detail in their lives is out of place. For them I have all of the answers. But I couldn't even keep my own marriage together. And I couldn't even mourn it properly because I'm the rock. I'm the one who keeps everything together for everyone."

"So what you're saying is that *you* need a rock?"

"I'd love to have one," I said, wiping my tears away as she jotted more notes down.

"Interesting," she said. "And what is your fantasy?"

I thought long and hard on that question. Of course the generic answers came up first: a threesome, sex on the beach, a romantic getaway. But none of them were things that I'd ever dreamed of doing. In reality I'd been so wrapped up in the lives of my friends and focusing on beating my disease, I'd lost track of myself. What did I like? What did I love? I didn't know. So I for sure didn't know what my fantasy was anymore.

"I don't know. I haven't thought about it."

After the words were out of my mouth, I wasn't able to read Madam Freya's facial expression anymore. I couldn't tell if she was disappointed by the answer or if she felt sorry for me. She scribbled some more in the notepad, and I wished I could see what she was writing. When she was finished, she looked at me with a seriousness in her eyes.

"I'm sorry," she said.

"What, is something wrong?"

"Yes. Unfortunately, you don't have a fantasy." The serious expression on her face was replaced with a smile. "And we have to fix that. You're going to Fantasy Island in the morning."

It held more secrets than I ever could in one lifetime. . . .

Chapter 29

Dez

Sleep was something that hadn't come easy to me that night. As I lay in bed, I checked in with my friends through texts. After, I tried to get some rest, but it was hard. It wasn't just that my body was still a little sore from the altercation, but I was beyond intrigued by what Madam Freya had told me. It all felt like a dream, but I was a strong believer that things didn't just happen. I was exactly where I needed to be. I had no idea what Fantasy Island would be like, but a big part of me felt like Madam Freya had barely even covered the surface. Eventually, as my mind raced, my eyes grew heavy, and my thoughts turned to dreams.

I felt like I'd only been asleep for a few seconds when I heard the sound of my alarm going off. I moaned and stretched before opening my eyes. Once I did, I was shocked to see sunshine peeking through the window. So shocked that I had to look at the digital clock on the nightstand beside me. It read eight in the morning.

"What the . . ." I mumbled.

I shook my head to completely wake myself up and hopped out of the bed. Madam Freya informed me the night before to be packed and ready to go by nine. That night of rest had done my body good, and I wasn't nearly as sore. And the hot water in the shower I took made me feel even better. I dressed in a pair of jean shorts and a pink halter top and put my hair in a ponytail. Shortly after setting my bags by the entrance to the suite, I heard a loud banging on it. I looked through the peephole and saw a man dressed in island attire standing on the other side. Skeptical, I stepped back from the door.

"Can I help you?"

"Good morning, ma'am! Madam Freya sent me to escort you to your transportation."

"Where is she? Madam Freya, I mean. I thought she'd be the one to escort me this morning. Not . . . you."

"She is attending to other guests, but I assure you that you are safe with me," the man said, but I still wasn't buying it.

"How do I know that?"

"She told me that you might behave this way. She has instructed me to tell you that she left a Taser in the drawer next to the refrigerator. I give you full permission to use it on me if you feel uncomfortable."

I went to the kitchen, briefly remembering Madam Freya going into the kitchen of the suite for something right before she left last night. After finding the Taser where the man said I would, I now knew why.

Going back to the door, I opened it, holding the Taser in view. However, the weapon in my hand didn't seem to stop the smile on the man's face from spreading.

"Aww, Miss Vincent. Pleased to meet you. I'm Peter."

"Nice to meet you."

He was a tall man about ten years my senior and balding at the top of his head. He seemed to have a bubbly personality and to be very helpful, which I found out when he pointed to my bags.

"If you are ready to go, I'll take these."

I stepped out of his way so that he could pick them up, and I followed him into the hallway. He led me to the elevator, and once we were on the main floor, he took me to the back exit of the resort, which led to the beach. Once outside, I took off my sandals as we walked in the sand. It was cool underneath my toes since the surrounding trees offered up so much shade. Peter pointed and directed me to look in front of us. "That is your ride right there!"

I followed his finger to a white seaplane perched on the water. In the distance I saw about five others getting on it.

"We have to fly?" I was confused.

"Surely you didn't think you could get to Fantasy Island by car. It's an *island,* dear. One only a few know how to get to."

"This is crazy," I said, stopping in my tracks. "I can't believe I'm about to do this."

"Madam Freya also said you might get cold feet. So she told me to give you this." Peter pulled something from his pocket and placed it in the palm of my hand.

When he let it go, I saw that it was a small rock. I stared at it for a while, shifting its weight in my hand. When I looked back at him, he gave a small nod.

"She said to tell you, 'Find your rock.'"

I looked back down at the gray stone and smiled when I realized what she had meant when she said I told her my fantasy. At the time I was so wrapped up in the motions that I failed to understand what she meant. But now I did. I smiled at Peter and nodded.

"Okay."

He walked me the remainder of the way to the plane and stowed my bags. Remembering I was still holding the Taser, I tucked it away in the fanny pack on my waist. The pilot of the plane helped me aboard, and I took a seat next to a young man. He was white, and from the alluring smell of his cologne and the expensive watch on his arm, I could only assume he was rolling in money.

"Thank you!" I called out to Peter, and he waved before heading back the way we came.

I took the time to eye the other passengers on the plane. There were six of us in total: four women and two men. The other guy was sitting behind me. He was young, Latino, and flamboyant as all get-out. I didn't even need to hear him talk to know he was the whole gay package. But as it was, the moment he saw me get on the plane, he couldn't help but run his mouth.

"Oh, my God! Your hair is laid, baby. Okay, baby hairs!" he said, leaning forward.

"Thank you."

"What's your name, sweetheart?"

"Dez."

"That's cute. I'm Paulie."

"Ugh, how much longer do we have to wait until we take off?" the man next to me groaned.

"Oop, sounds like Tyler can't wait to get his dick sucked," Paulie said with a chuckle.

"For twenty thousand dollars I better get more than that!" Tyler exclaimed.

"Twe . . . Did you just say twenty thousand dollars?" I asked, astonished at the steep fee. "That's how much it costs to go to this Fantasy Island? I thought it was invitation only."

"It is. You get invited, and you pay the fee when you accept. If you're on the plane with us, you should know this," Tyler noted and raised a brow at me.

"Somebody paid my fee," I said, pursing my lips and tapping my chin. "I guess."

"Lucky you. You get to get fucked on someone else's dime!" Paulie said.

"Well, I don't know if I would pay twenty thousand dollars to get fucked. Have either of you been there before?" I asked, turning so I could see both of them.

"Unfortunately, I'm a Fantasy Island virgin," Paulie told me. "I got my invitation from my older whore of a sister. She came a few years ago and hasn't stopped talking about it. Nobody believed her, of course. But that's her fault. She pops pills like Tic Tacs."

"But you're here, so that means you believed her," I pointed out.

"Of course I believed her. She's my sister!"

"Oookaay. Anyways, what about you?" I turned my attention on Tyler.

"Never been. But my uncle has. My invitation came from him."

"Did either of them tell you guys what it's like?"

"All my uncle said is that his wildest dreams came true. It's where he met my aunt."

"So it's more than living out a sexual fantasy?"

"It's whatever you want it to be, honey," Paulie butted in. "But I, for one, am not wasting a week-long fuck fest on finding love. I want to have a ball with some balls against mine, okay? Shit, I might even try some pussy."

"Any other day hearing some shit like that might make me gag. But today? I might just want to watch." Tyler shrugged and then winked at me. "What happens on the island stays on the island."

"What package did you choose, Dez?" Paulie asked me, and I could tell that he was genuinely interested.

"I haven't decided yet. I'm interested to know what the Euphoria package is. It sounds—"

"Like drugs. Uh-uh. Nope. Choose a different one. You seem like a nice girl. You don't need to turn into a drug fiend on vacation!"

By then the pilot and his copilot had gotten back on the plane. I turned my body forward facing and fastened my seat belt. As we prepared to embark on our journey, Paulie's words replayed in my head. *Drugs?* Well, Madam Freya did say whatever a person wanted, they could have, and I was sure they didn't draw the line at some drugs.

When the pilot took off, I found myself gripping the seat. I'd been on a seaplane before, and it was my least favorite flight experience. Something about a small plane over a huge body of water just didn't sit right with me. Paulie went to talk to the other ladies on the plane, and Tyler focused his attention out of the window. I decided to take a page out of his book and peer out of the window. The higher we got in the sky, the more visible the island became. The blue of the ocean was calm and serene. It held more secrets than I ever could in one lifetime. After about thirty minutes, I noticed a gigantic chunk of land surrounded by the ocean. The closer we got, the bigger it seemed to be. The many tall trees made it look beautiful and green. I knew we'd reached our destination even before we started to descend. My heart felt like it was about to thump out of my chest, and I tried to will any nervous thoughts away. If my friends knew what I was doing, they would probably have a heart attack. We'd done many spontaneous things, but none like what I was about to do. I honestly hadn't even made up my mind if I would truly partake. But why not?

Once the pilot landed, he got on the mic and turned to face us. "All right, people! We've reached our destination. Fantasy Island welcomes you! Oh, what a treasure awaits you."

It's our pleasure to pleasure you. . . .

Chapter 30

Dez

"Oh. *Oh!*" The shocked voice belonged to me.

After landing, we were met by two guides and split up into two different trolley cars. I stuck with Paulie and Tyler. Our guide drove us up a trail to, I could only assume, the big dome I'd seen when I was in the air. On our way, plain as day for everyone to see, was a couple under a tree. The man was standing with his pants around his ankles. The woman, a long-haired brunette, was on her knees and nearly swallowing his dick whole. The guide barely batted an eye at the sighting, but Paulie, Tyler, and I gawked.

"Goddamn," Tyler said as he watched the guy get the head of his lifetime.

"She knows what she's doing," I commented. "That thing is big, too."

As we continued to drive, I saw many other couples outside in nature getting it on and having the time of their lives. And they weren't all straight. I saw many gay and lesbian couples as well. I couldn't believe it. I had never seen so many people having sex in one setting in my life. It was like an orgy outside.

"Public sex is on a lot of our guests' fantasy list," our guide told us. She was an older woman, maybe in her early fifties. "If that's something you like, you'll fit right in."

"Sign me up. I'm ready to make all of my fantasies come to life, right now!" Paulie said eagerly.

"I'm sure you are, and you'll be able to as soon as you speak to your counselor."

"Counselor?" I asked.

"Yes. Sometimes people come here and ask for things that might be too extreme for them. We want to make sure that the packages they choose are a right fit."

"Makes sense." I nodded.

"Where are you taking us, ma'am?" Tyler asked.

"To the City of Dreams, of course."

"Is that the dome I saw when we were in the plane?"

"The dome covers the perimeter of the city. It keeps out unwanted animals and protects against storms. See?"

She pointed ahead of us, and I saw that we had reached our destination. The dome went up farther than my eyes could see and was translucent. There was a large opening in it that allowed us to drive through and enter the city. I tried not to think about how all of that had gotten there. It would just make my head hurt. Instead, I just enjoyed the moment and the scenery.

Once we entered the dome, I was blown away because it was really like a city. I half expected to see people having sex outside all of the buildings, but there weren't. Our guide drove us past several buildings. What I noticed was that there were four main buildings, each with a different-color plaque outside of it. Connected to each individual building were several smaller buildings. It intrigued me, especially watching people eagerly enter them. I wondered where they were going. Suddenly, the vehicle stopped when we had driven a little ways from the color buildings, and we were stopped outside some sort of resort.

"This is where you'll meet your counselors," our guide said. "Once you put your fantasy package together, you'll be directed to which color house you'll be staying in. Grab your things and go inside. You're expected."

We got out and grabbed our things. Tyler led the way inside. Instantly, I felt the cool air, which was a relief since it had been so hot outside. A stunning woman with green eyes and freckles stood in front of the revolving doors. Those features wouldn't have stood out if she weren't a black woman. Her long hair was pulled into a bun, and she wore a big smile and a red skirt suit that hugged every curve. In her hands she was holding a golden clipboard with the matching pen.

"Welcome to Fantasy Island, where it's our pleasure to pleasure you. I'm Mena, and I'm here to make sure all of your needs are met and also to make sure they're right for you. Names please?"

"Tyler."

"Paulie, baby!"

"Desiree."

"Great. If the three of you will please follow me to my office . . ."

We followed her through the elaborate building and passed many golden statues of animals. I didn't need to wonder if it was real gold because I was sure it was. The building wasn't quiet, due to other people being there, and I assumed it was headquarters of the small city. I passed an Arabic woman pouting and throwing a fit to a man holding a clipboard. It very much resembled the one Mena was holding, so I guessed he too was a counselor.

"Please! I want to change my package. I thought I wanted to feel the delicate touch of a woman, and it was great, but now I miss the strength of a man. Actually, I want both at the same time! Please switch me to the black building!"

I didn't get to hear what the counselor said back to her, because Mena turned us down a long hall. When we finally reached her office, she motioned toward two chairs outside of it and looked at Tyler and me.

"Please have a seat. I will talk to you each one-on-one."

I obliged and sat down in one of the comfortable seats, noting how good it felt under my bottom. Paulie followed Mena in the office, and I couldn't help but to smirk at his walk. His switch was more vicious than mine. He winked at us right before Mena shut the door. Not knowing how long they would be, I pulled out my phone and prepared to send my girls another message.

"Dammit! No service," I groaned.

"I'm not surprised in a place like this. To keep things as secretive as possible, we'll probably be stripped of our phones altogether," Tyler said.

He was right. I couldn't think of how else Fantasy Island had stayed under wraps. A place like that would be a hot commodity in the modern world. It wouldn't be as special. Time seemed to tick on by, and when Paulie finally reemerged, I didn't know how long it had been. He was all smiles walking out of Mena's office. In his hands he was holding a purple key card. He grabbed his luggage and blew Tyler and me a kiss.

"Well, I'm off to fulfill my fantasy. Maybe I'll see you two around."

We waved him off, and he was gone. Next, Mena called Tyler into the room, and I sighed. I was hoping I'd be next. I sank down in my chair and got lost in my mind again. I thought back to the packages I'd seen and tried to decide which one would best suit me. The Mandingo package? An image of a gigantic penis sliding in and out of me flashed in my head, and I quickly shook it away. I wanted my lady parts to still be intact after the trip, so that was out of the question. I wished the other packages went more into detail about what they entailed, but I was sure that was what Mena was for.

After some time, the door to the office opened again. Tyler exited, holding a red key card in his hand. He had a mischievous grin on his face, and I could only guess that he'd put together the perfect fantasy for himself.

"I'll see you around," he said to me as he grabbed his things.

"Have fun," I told him.

He walked away, leaving me alone with Mena. She gave me a curious look as she motioned me inside of her office. I cleared my throat and stood up, leaving my luggage behind. Once inside of her office, Mena sat behind her desk, and I sat in the chair in front of it. The seat was still warm from

Tyler and Paulie. Mena glanced at her laptop briefly and then at the clipboard in front of her before looking at me.

"Okay, first things first. Here is our Wi-Fi code," she said and pointed to the wall where a board with the word "Hippopotamus" hung. "Check in with any friends and family, and let them know you're safe but you want to enjoy a quiet vacation."

"Okay," I said and did what I was told. It took a few moments to send the messages, but when I was done, I looked back at her. "Done."

"Good. Now give me your phone." She held her hand out, and when I failed to follow instructions that time, she chuckled. "A place like this can't stay a secret in the sights of a cell phone. They aren't allowed on the island. I'm sure you understand. You will get it back the day you leave."

"Okay," I sighed and reluctantly gave her my phone.

She took it and put it in her drawer. After that, a short-lived silence pierced the room. She went back to staring at me. Her gaze traveled from my eyes to my lips and to my cleavage. It lingered there briefly before coming back to my eyes.

"Well, this doesn't happen very often," she said lightheartedly.

"What doesn't?"

"Usually I have something to go on to help build a guest's perfect experience. But you seem to be a surprise visitor."

"Yeah, I—"

"No need to explain, Desiree. I was already informed of the circumstances." She gave me a kind smile. "Actually, I'm kind of excited to help build something from scratch. So let's get to it, shall we?"

"Okay," I said and tried to force myself to loosen up. "So how do we do this? Do you just ask me what my ideal fantasy is?"

"If only it were that easy. See, when you just go head-on like that, you usually get a two-dimensional answer. A woman will say she wants a threesome. But what she leaves out is that simultaneously she really wants a dick shoved down her throat, one in her ass, and one in her pussy, stroking her G-spot, all while having her nipples worshipped. And that's not a threesome, is it? It becomes much more than that."

"Wow. That's intense."

"Very. So let us get the basics out of the way. Are you straight?"

"Yes."

"Curious?" On that question she glanced up at me.

I could have been wrong, but I felt like she was eager to know my answer to that question. "I've had sex with women, in college."

"Is it an experience you'd like to have again?"

"Umm, sure?"

"Yes or no answers only please, Desiree."

"Fine, then yes."

"Perfect. Do you prefer small, average, large, or oversized penises?"

"Large, but nothing extreme," I answered.

"Noted. Does the thought of participating in an orgy excite or repel you?"

"Neither," I said and then thought more deeply about the question. "I wouldn't mind having my body worshipped."

"By how many people at a time?" The seriousness in her voice almost threw me off, but then I remembered that she was serious as a heart attack.

"Two at the most."

"What sounds more desirable, sex indoors or outdoors?"

"Both."

"Public or private?"

"Private."

"Are you into anal sex?"

"Yes."

"Do you prefer to give or receive?" Mena asked as she scribbled words onto her clipboard.

"Both will make me orgasm."

"Any preference on race?"

I almost told her I preferred black men only, but I stopped myself. Mainly that was all I'd ever had. And the women I'd slept with were black as well. When I hesitated, Mena looked up at me, and I smiled.

"Desiree?"

"No, no preference. As long as they're easy on the eyes."

"And last but not least, what's your fantasy, Desiree?" Mena asked and tapped her chin with her pen. The curious look had come back to her eyes. Her gaze felt warm on my face.

"I thought you just said that you get two-dimensional answers when you ask that head-on."

"Something tells me that you might surprise me."

"I don't think I will, because I don't think I have a fantasy. But I love to have orgasms, and I love to arrive at that destination by different paths every time."

"So what would your ideal path be to your next climax if you could choose?" Mena asked, biting her pen.

It was then that I took notice of how perfect and full her heart-shaped lips were. The red lipstick she wore was slightly moist at the opening of her mouth, where her tongue rested on the pen. Her green eyes stared intensely at me, making my breathing shallow. I swallowed the spit in my mouth, not wanting to read the room wrong, and blinked my eyes.

"If I could choose, I would—" I stopped abruptly when an intrusive vision came to my mind.

It was of Mena and me. She'd knocked everything on her desk off and was between my legs, devouring me like the Last Supper. The next image was of us in the scissors position, grinding passionately and mixing our juices to an explosive climax. In real time I felt my clit swell as my eyes fell to her cleavage. I found myself wondering what color her nipples were and if she liked them licked or nibbled on.

When I finally caught myself, I cleared my throat. I was surprised at myself. I hadn't had an unsavory thought about a woman since my wild college days. But there was something about Mena that was alluring, which probably was why she was good at her job.

"Are you okay, Desiree?"

"Yeah. Yes. Um, if I could choose my next path to an orgasm, I would just like it to be in the rain. I would love to feel the cool drops of water stimulating my body while I'm being pleased."

"That's it? You don't have any ideal partner, or partners?"

"No. I'm here to experience a fantasy, why does it have to be one I come up with? Surprise me."

My answer brought a slow smile to Mena's lips. She nodded and scribbled a few more things down before she reached in her drawer. From it, she pulled a thick black key card.

"I think the best thing for you will be the Euphoria package. Every day will be something new and exciting." She handed me the key card. "This is your activity card. You'll be taken to the black building, and you'll be staying in room 313. Just go with the flow of things. Goodbye, Desiree. Your fantasy awaits."

Things get really steamy in the spa rooms. . . .

Chapter 31

Dez

The black building was just that: black. Everything inside was absolutely breathtaking. With each step my feet took on the crystalized granite floors, I felt more and more at ease. There were many people wandering the halls, and although some were holding on to each other tightly, none were doing anything extremely risqué. Maybe a deep tongue kiss here and there, but that was it. They were all colors, shapes, and sizes.

I'd entered through the main entrance, but I soon realized that it branched off to all of the other smaller buildings attached to it. In the air I smelled delicious food, so I could only guess there was some sort of restaurant inside. I'd just have to find it. First, I needed to drop my things off at the room. I followed the signs that led me to room 313, and they took me to a bunch of elevators. However, on the way, I passed a digital board on the wall. Curious, I stopped to read it.

"'The next euphoric check-in: noon,'" I said aloud.

"Have you been?"

The voice caught me off guard, and when I turned around, I was met with a charming smile. It belonged to a handsome Asian man with a muscular build. His olive skin seemed to have a tan, and he was shirtless, like he'd just come from the beach. When I didn't say anything, he looked down and saw my luggage. He shook his head sheepishly.

"You just got here. Of course you haven't been."

"I'm almost scared to ask what it is," I spoke finally. "Is it some sort of huge orgy or something?"

"No," he laughed. "That's more something the green building would do. We have more of a respectable ambiance here. More discreet."

"So what is it then?"

"It's . . . Actually, you'll find out."

"Will you be there?"

"Maybe," he chuckled. "It just depends."

"On what?"

"You'll see."

"Mm-hmm, what's your name anyway?"

"How rude of me," he said and held out his hand. "Andrew, but my friends call me Andy."

"And are we friends?" I asked, shaking his hand.

"I hope we can be," he said, caressing my knuckles with his thumb.

"We'll see. I'm Dez, short for Desiree."

"Do you need help to your room?"

"I think I can manage. Thank you though, Andy." I winked at him and continued on my way.

"Dez?" I heard him call, and I turned back around. He was holding up his black key card. "Check the room number on your key card at noon."

Before I could say anything else, he went on about his business. Not sure what he meant, I looked back down at my key card. I hadn't noticed it before, but there was a digital message on it that said, Welcome to Euphoria. I wondered if the message would change.

I finally made my way up the elevator and to my room, which turned out to be another small suite. I had a nice view of the island, and thankfully nobody outside was getting their back blown out. There was a fridge inside the room that was thankfully stocked with yogurt and fruit, which I gladly ate after I stored my luggage. When I was done, I found myself staring at the bed, wanting badly to crawl under the covers and go to sleep.

"No, Dez. You've come this far. You need to experience what this island has to offer. You need it," I said to myself.

Looking at the clock beside the bed, I saw that I only had one hour until noon. That was the time of the next check-in. I had no idea what was in store, but apparently I was going to find out. I rushed to find something sexy to wear in my suitcase and opted for a black two-piece skirt set. The top looked more like a bikini and made my boobs perk up perfectly. The skirt stopped right under my round bottom. Anyone around me while I was wearing that might not be able to keep their hands off of me.

I hopped in the shower, and after that, I touched up my hair. By the time I was dressed and ready, it was ten minutes until noon. I sprayed some perfume on myself and sat on the bed like an eager schoolgirl with my hands clasped together. The key card was in my lap, and I kept glancing down feverishly at it. At exactly noon, it vibrated, and the message on it changed. I held it up so I could read it clearly.

Spa 5.

I didn't know where the spa was, but I was sure I'd be able to find it. Or ask someone for directions. I took a deep breath and slid on my sandals before grabbing my key card. When I left my room, it was then that I realized asking someone for directions was out of the question. It was like a madhouse, everyone rushing in every direction to get to where they were supposed to be. I saw a little bit of everything. Whips and chains, masquerade masks, character cosplay, even complete nudity. The only thing I could do was hurry so I could be the next to get on the elevators.

There was nothing but excitement and giggles in the air. I couldn't lie, I was growing anxious. Something about not knowing what was in store for me made me smile. When finally there was a ding and two of the elevator doors opened, I quickly got on one before it was full. When the doors closed, I realized I was standing next to a completely naked man. He was white, and when I looked down, I saw that he already had a rock-hard erection. My eyes found his face, and he was grinning down at me.

"Glory hole. I can't wait," he said.

"Sounds fun," was all I could think to say back to him.

"You should join in if tonight's fantasy isn't fitting. I would love to cum all inside of a chocolate thing like you." He raised his eyebrows up and down at me.

"Jonothan, leave her alone!" a woman on the opposite side of him said. She had a thick Australian accent. "All the dicks here, I'm sure she isn't interested in yours."

When the elevator stopped again, it cleared out, leaving only me and the woman who had spoken up. She was a short, petite thing with a long ponytail. She was dressed in a cheerleader getup and had the pom-poms to match. I must have looked like I was unsure if I should get off too, because the woman turned to me.

"Do you know where you're going?" she asked.

"Um, to spa five?"

"Oh. *Ohhh.*" The woman raised her brows.

"What? Should I get off here?"

"Nope, we're going to the main floor," she said and pressed the button to close the elevator doors. "I'm going to the weight room, and it's right next to the spa. I'll show you."

"Thank you. I'm Dez, by the way."

"I'm Kira," she said and eyed me up and down. "You're beautiful. Is it your first time here?"

"To Fantasy Island? Yes. I've never been."

"It's my third time on the island. First time doing the Euphoria package though. I've had a blast so far. I was in spa room three yesterday. Whew, what a time."

"What happens?"

"For you? I don't know," she told me as the elevator came to a stop and the doors opened. She motioned for me to follow her, which I did. "Everyone's fantasy session is different. They're based on the bio sheet you sent in, plus whatever your counselor thinks will fit you. After that, you're paired with others who match. Each fantasy is a different adventure."

"Bio sheet?" I asked, and Kira stopped in her tracks.

"You didn't send in a bio sheet?"

"No, I actually am kind of here spontaneously."

"Wow, so your counselor is pulling all of the strings here. Fun!" Kira's eyes brightened. "Well, just so you know, if you like a specific fantasy or person more than the rest, let your counselor know so you can relive it as many times as you can while you're here."

We walked down a long hallway that led to another building. On the way, we passed a cafeteria with many different options of food to eat. It all looked delicious to me. I almost said, "Forget the spa," and went to eat. But I stayed on course. When we reached our destination, I saw the entrance to the gym, and Kira pointed me to where the spa rooms were a little ways away. The first thing I noticed was that part of the black building was empty.

"Where is everybody?"

"In their fantasies of course. Euphoria is a private experience for guests on Fantasy Island. Like me, I get to have the whole gym with some sexy hunk. I always wanted to be fucked by a football coach, and I *love* to be dominated by big men."

"Anything else you can tell me?"

"Just that things get really steamy in the spa rooms." Kira winked at me and then skipped away to the gym.

You want some more strawberries? . . .

Chapter 32

Dez

Spa room five was dimly lit by candles when I walked inside. It wasn't a huge room, but it was big enough. On one side there was a bucket of ice and a bottle of champagne chilling inside. Next to it was a tray of strawberries. To my utter surprise, I heard Jagged Edge playing softly from an unseen speaker. I smiled. All of it was my favorite combination, but how could Mena have known that? I assumed she was the one behind it since she was my counselor, after all.

The greatest thing that caught my eye, above all, was the sexy chocolate man standing next to the massage table. He wasn't wearing anything but a towel over his oiled-up body. He didn't speak any words. He just held his hand out to me. I walked slowly over to him and took his hand. When I did, he pulled me into his strong arms. I liked that. I liked it a lot. His body smelled of a gentle cologne, and his breath was minty. My heart rate quickened, and I felt my knees weaken. I tried to think of the last time I'd been with anyone, and my mind went blank. I didn't know what to do or say. *Should I introduce myself? Should we remain a mystery?* I felt like a virgin all over again.

"This is all new to me. I've never done this before," I whispered up at him.

"Don't worry about a thing," he said in a low, deep voice, looking me deeply in the eyes. "We got you."

"We?" I asked, but the second the question was out of my mouth, I felt someone come up behind me.

Against my butt cheeks, I felt a hard erection. I turned my head and saw another man fine as wine. He was much younger than me but old enough to get this work. He was so light skinned that he could pass as white, especially with his fiery red hair. However, it was the texture of that very hair that gave him away and told me he had some black in him. Well, his hair and the size of his dick. I found myself reaching down in front and back of me. I didn't stop until I was grasping both of their third legs in my hands. A small moan fell from my lips, and I could feel my clit jump in excitement.

"What are you going to do to me?" I asked.

"Everything," Red Hair said.

Chocolate—that was what I was going to call him for now—turned my head back to him and kissed me deeply. I welcomed his tongue in my mouth and kissed him back. Behind me, Red Hair dropped to his knees and massaged the back of my thighs, working his hands up to my butt. Once there, he lifted my skirt up and pulled my thong down. His strong hands parted my cheeks, and his tongue went to work elsewhere. While he was devouring my ass, Chocolate reached down and played with my swollen clit, swirling his middle finger in a circular motion around it.

"Ooh!" I cried out and broke our kiss. It was all feeling too good.

Red Hair stood back up and turned me around to face him. He scooped me up in his arms and laid me down gently on the massage table. Their hands went to work and completely undressed me. When I was completely naked, they removed their towels from their waists. The sight of their erections made me lift my legs and open them wide. My own hand found its way to my pussy, and I slipped two fingers inside. They watched me and stroked themselves watching me finger fuck myself.

"Damn, girl. That thing is leaking," Chocolate moaned and positioned himself between my legs.

He removed my fingers and replaced them with his own, wrapping his lips around my clit. The way he licked and sucked on it, you would have thought it was a Bomb Pop. His fingers made the "come here" motion inside of me and tickled my G-spot. Red Hair had disappeared for a moment, but when he returned, he had a strawberry and the bottle of champagne in his hands. In between my cries of pleasure, he fed me the strawberry. It was so sweet on my tongue, and the more I ate, the more I wanted something else in my mouth. I grabbed him by the dick and guided it to my mouth.

"Fuck!" he exclaimed in surprise when it went to the back of my throat and I didn't gag.

I slurped and sucked his dick like a pro while Chocolate was bringing me to my first orgasm. My back arched when I felt the buildup, and it slammed back down on the massage table when it released. I squirted my juices all over Chocolate, and he tried his best to slurp them all up.

"Shit," I heard myself say with the tip of Red Hair's dick on my lips.

Chocolate stood up and disappeared from my sights for a second, when he came back, he was sliding a condom on. He repositioned himself in between my legs, and Red Hair poured champagne on my breasts for Chocolate to lick off, which he did gladly. While Chocolate was nibbling and playing with my nipples, Red Hair poured some champagne in my mouth. I drank it and went back to pleasuring him. When Chocolate positioned his tip at my opening, I got excited and began jacking Red Hair off as I sucked.

I felt electricity jolt through my body when Chocolate slid in the first time, and all of our moans filled the air. He gave me a few slow strokes before picking up the speed. All the while, Red Hair made sure to keep my nipples stimulated by pinching them. I stared up at his turned-on face and could feel his dick jumping in my mouth from excitement. He was thoroughly enjoying watching Chocolate fuck the shit out of me. I couldn't lie, my juices were on a steady flow. I'd never experienced two men at the same time, and it was marvelous.

When Red Hair couldn't just watch anymore, the men switched places. He put a condom on and flipped me over so he could get it from the back. When he pierced me, I could instantly feel a difference between the two men. Not in size, but in their stroke. He was more gentle with his thrusts, enjoying every second of this pussy. I was able to match his strokes, even when Chocolate shoved his dick down my throat. He didn't want me to be in charge of sucking it how I wanted. He wanted to fuck my face, and it was a good thing I didn't have a gag reflex. Both men were digging into me relentlessly, and the only thing that could be heard were the "gawk gawk" sounds coming from my mouth paired with the macaroni-and-cheese stir coming from my cat. Oh, and of course their whimpers of pleasure.

Behind me I could feel Red Hair struggling to keep his footing, and in front of me I could see Chocolate's knees wobbling. I felt powerful. Without warning, Chocolate pulled himself from my throat, and Red Hair stopped fucking me. Chocolate lifted me up and wrapped my legs around him. I thought he was going to do me in the air, but he surprised me by lying down on the massage table with me on top of him. When I saw Red Hair step to the side and put some oil on his dick, I knew what was about to happen. I took a deep breath.

I'd never done double penetration before, not even with a toy. But there was no better time for a first time. I arched my back the best I could so that both of them would have easy entry. Chocolate penetrated me first, and I didn't wince, but when Red Hair slid his tip in my anus, I sucked air quickly through my teeth.

"There's a good girl," he coached me through. "Look at you taking this dick. You've been taking both of our dicks so good. You got it, baby."

"Uhnnnn!" I cried when he eased the rest in.

I continued to cry out as they began stroking at the same time. In seconds the pain turned into a pleasure that went beyond my body. I lost track of how many and the different kinds of orgasms I had. I just knew I had to be in heaven. Either heaven or at a theme park riding my favorite ride.

I didn't want it to end, but it had to. They couldn't hold their climax back forever. Red Hair came first, I felt him jerking behind me like he was having a seizure. He pulled out and with trembling hands removed the condom so he could rub his nut out onto my jiggling butt cheeks.

Chocolate was next, but he didn't pull out. He shouted loudly in my ear, and I felt him jumping violently inside of me as he released into his condom. His hands gripped my back tight until his peak was over. And when it was, his body went limp. I caught my breath on top of him and then climbed off. Red Hair helped me regain my footing. It was the craziest thing. These two men had just explored the depths of my body, but I was too shy to look him in the face. He gently grabbed my chin and made me look up at him. There were a few sweat beads falling from his forehead, but his smile was infectious. I didn't know what to say, but he did.

"You want some more strawberries?"

It's raining. . . .

Chapter 33

Dez

"Wait, wait!" My shouts filled the air.

I waved my hands at the man preparing to mount me. It was my second day there on Fantasy Island, and I was in the middle of my second fantasy. That evening I was in the gym, and it was my turn to role-play. My guy for the moment was a muscular white man who put me in the mind of Channing Tatum. He was dressed as Tarzan, and I was Jane. *Tarzan* had been one of my favorite movies even as an adult. I thought a rough, wild man making love to a damsel in distress was sexy and romantic. But I couldn't shake one thought from my mind. *How* had Mena known?

I could have chalked the strawberries, champagne, and music from the day before up to chance. But this couldn't have been a coincidence, I was sure. It was on my mind so hard that I couldn't even get into the fantasy. I stood up from the cot made of fake branches and leaves.

"Is something wrong? Did I do something you don't like?" Fake Tarzan asked with his dick just swinging.

"No, no. It's not you. It's just . . . I have to go."

I felt bad for running off like that, but I didn't know what else to do. I left the gym still dressed in my costume, but I didn't go to my room. I stopped at the café to get some water and to sit down. The women and men working didn't even bat an eye at my getup. I was just handed my water glass and a menu in case I got hungry.

I sat down by the window and sipped my water. My thoughts went to Mena as I stared outside at the budding storm. What was Mena up to? Was she truly trying to give me a great experience on the island or was she completely trying to screw with my mind? That wasn't all. Last night, after I'd gone back to my room, I was still overstimulated. I masturbated, but I wasn't thinking about what had just happened to me. The visual playing in my mind was the same one I had when I was sitting in her office. The one of us on her desk making love. My sheets were soaking wet by the time I was done. And that was another reason I couldn't get all the way into my fantasy with Tarzan. I sighed and took another sip of my water.

"Is this seat taken?" a voice asked.

It was Andy, the Asian man I'd met when I'd first arrived. I smiled and shook my head, gesturing for him to sit. He was dressed casually and had a plate of eggrolls in his hands. It smelled delicious. He noticed me staring and offered me one.

"You know the food is free here, right?" he joked, watching me scarf the eggroll down.

"I know, I just didn't know I was hungry until I smelled your food," I told him, taking my last bite. "Why are you here anyway? I thought almost everybody would be in a fantasy right now."

"I could say the same about you," he said with a smirk.

"I was just in one. I left early."

"Not into it?"

"I was, just not with him."

"I see," he said.

I looked away, but I could feel his eyes burning a hole in the side of my face. Even as he ate, he kept his eyes on me. If I weren't so chocolate, I would have blushed.

"What?" I finally asked, turning back to him.

"I'm sure you hear this all the time, but you are stunning."

"I do hear it often, but it never gets old," I joked.

"Tell me about yourself, Dez. Who are you? What do you do? What do you like?"

For the next thirty minutes, Andy and I sat sharing information back and forth. He learned that I was a teacher from Atlanta and I enjoyed to travel. I felt like I talked a little too much about Bali, but it was my favorite place, and I couldn't get over how beautiful the water was there. I made him promise me that he'd go visit one day.

To my surprise, Andy told me that he was a very successful businessman and that he'd been referred to Fantasy Island to get the stick out of his butt. I thought that was funny, because to me, he seemed laid-back. But I guessed that would happen when you were getting fucked right every single day.

"When do you leave?" I asked.

"Tomorrow actually."

"Oh, wow, in the middle of the week?"

"Yes. I have some important business to take care of. Plus, now I need to plan for my Bali trip," he said with a wink. He stood up from the table and held a card out to me. "I would really love to get to know you more. When you get home, look me up. And, Dez?"

"Yeah?"

"Remember this is just a place to form your deepest desires. Some you might have just realized. You don't have to just take what's given to you. Live a little."

I smiled as I watched him walk away. I smiled even harder when I saw that he left me two more eggrolls. I ate them up and went up to my room. I told myself that I was going to take Andy's advice. After I changed my clothes, I was going to go talk to Mena and take control of my experience. Was that what I wanted to do, or did I really want to ask her how she knew anything about me? Or did I want to—

Knock! Knock!

I hadn't even had time to take my clothes off when there was a knock on my door. Peeking through the peephole, I raised my brows at who it was. I opened the door and stepped back, slightly embarrassed at my outfit.

"Mena. You must have known I was on my way to come see you."

Mena stood there, that day wearing a low-cut pink dress with her hair flowing over her shoulders. I waved my hand, letting her know it was okay for her to come in and shut the door. She looked around like she hadn't seen probably a hundred rooms just like it, before turning to face me. Her eyes hovered over the Jane costume before reaching my face.

"Is something wrong? Is that why you were coming to see me?" she asked.

"I was . . . Wait, why are you *here?*"

Her showing up so randomly had caught me so off guard that I hadn't even thought about why she was there. Until right that very moment, anyway. She seemed taken aback by my question, and she stuttered over her words, trying to find them. Finally, she stood straighter and pursed her lips.

"I was just coming to check to see how you were getting along after your first few days."

"It was fine. How did you know about the champagne and strawberries? And about Tarzan?"

"It's not hard to find out simple things about people on social media," she said like it wasn't a big deal. But it was.

"I'm rarely on social media. You would have had to scroll a long time to find out those small but important details about someone. Most wouldn't put in that much effort to find out things about someone."

"All that matters is that you enjoyed yourself," she said with a straight face.

She was almost believable. Almost. But I could tell that she was *trying* not to show emotion on her face. Someone being truthful wouldn't need to try. They would just do.

"Do you usually go through such great lengths to make sure your guests have an enjoyable experience on the island?"

"You were a special case. You had no bio sheet to go off of."

"Uh-huh. Is it standard practice to go around checking on your guests?"

"Like I said, you were a special case," Mena blurted out quickly. She was flustered. So flustered that she couldn't even give me eye contact. "Well, if you're good, I'll leave then."

She walked with a fast pace and tried to go around me, but my body moved before my mind could catch up. I grabbed her hand, stopping her in her place. She looked at my hand and slowly back into my eyes.

"Yesterday was great. But the strawberries and champagne were my favorite part," I started softly. "And today, I couldn't even do it because I couldn't stop thinking about how you knew what you knew. And then I found myself wondering when was the last time someone had even tried to figure out what I like. I know it's your job, but—"

"It's not. I mean, not that part. Once I input your information in the system, it automatically generates fantasies it thinks that you'll like. I guess I went a little beyond. I wanted you to enjoy your time and . . ."

"And what?" I asked when her voice trailed off. But she didn't say anything. I swallowed the lump in my throat and decided to tell her the truth. "Last night after my fantasy, I came back to my room. And I rubbed my clit until I came all over myself. I touched myself to the very first fantasy that came into my mind on this island."

"And what was that?" she breathed.

"Of you. Of us having nasty, passionate sex. And I don't think anything will suffice until I get that. As crazy as it sounds, I think you felt it too. So answer me this, Mena: men or women?"

"Women."

"Give or receive?"

"Both."

She took a step closer to me, but I shook my head. I led her to the sliding door in my room and opened it. She looked outside and smiled up at me with her beautiful green eyes. I didn't know if what I felt for her was lust or something else. But I was about to find out.

"It's raining," I said, returning her smile right before I pulled her outside.

Part Four

Fantasy Island: The Present

If being a wife to him meant not being true to myself, then the marriage wasn't worth it. . . .

Chapter 34

Roze

The time for our trip seemed to come in the blink of an eye. But then again, my life seemed to be racing by. I'd made the decision to not let Isaiah back into the house and to go forward with the divorce. Of course he tried to make amends, but the cuts were just too deep. It wasn't even just the cheating. I'd finally come to terms with the fact that I wasn't the woman for him. That didn't make me any less. It just meant I would never be able to fit into the shoes he had set out for his desired partner. I didn't want to, either. If being a wife to him meant not being true to myself, then the marriage wasn't worth it.

Now just because I was standing ten toes in my decision didn't make it any less hard to make. I still had the girls to think about, for one. And for two, the dynamic of my life was about to change forever. It had already changed. I'd grown accustomed to sleeping alone. However, I wasn't alone. Nina moved into the house with us. She said it was because she knew I'd need her to be more hands-on with the girls, but really I thought she just wanted to keep a close and caring eye on me. Whichever it was, I was grateful. Until the divorce was final, we would be working with one income.

With all of the changes going on in my home, it was hard to leave Aaliyah and Maya. They were going to stay home with Nina a few of the days and then go with Isaiah the remainder of the time I was gone. I knew they would be fine, but I would miss them.

My girls and I had decided once again to fly out of L.A., and I was the first one to the airport. My flight got in early, and all there was left to do was wait for Imani and Logan. While I did so, I found myself playing the video Dez made for us the summer before. It was so hard to keep the tears at bay. So hard to the point that I couldn't do it. It also probably didn't help that I played it over and over. We were really about to take our first Travelistas trip without her. All of our photos from there on out would contain only three. It was a tough pill to swallow. Mourning was probably one of the most challenging things I'd ever faced. It was like one day you were fine and the next you were a mess. There were no cheat codes to the healing process, or if there were, I hadn't found them yet.

For the first time, I had no idea what to expect on our vacation. Mainly because no matter how much research I'd done on Fantasy Island, I couldn't find anything. I couldn't believe I'd let Logan talk me into going to some fairy-tale place. No, it wasn't Logan. It was Dez. I was nervous and excited at the same time. What in the world was in store for us?

"I was watching that on repeat my whole flight here."

Logan's voice startled me. I looked up from my phone screen to see her standing there holding a Gucci bag and a neck pillow. Comfortably dressed, she was in a tan biker shorts outfit. She held her arms out to me, and I stood up to embrace her. The hug I gave was slightly tighter than I intended, but she returned the gesture. When we pulled apart, we sat next to each other and shared my blanket in the chilly airport.

"I don't know why I keep watching this damn thing. All I'm doing is making myself cry."

"Me too. I think we're crazy," she said, and we both laughed. "Let me guess. Mrs. Late is late."

"You know that girl likes to show up at the last minute," I said, giving Logan a knowing look.

"I hope she doesn't try to get out of coming."

"She better not!"

"Well, you know Kevin came and got all of his stuff on Wednesday."

"I did not know that," I said, raising a brow. "I was busy all this week with the girls. Oh, my God, I'm such a bad friend. How did she take it?"

"I think it made it real for her. I really thought they would bounce back from this, but he is so pissed at her. And that wasn't even the worst of it."

"What happened?"

"He served me with divorce papers," Imani's voice said, almost making me jump in my seat. "If y'all are going to talk about my business, at least wait until I'm here to talk about it with you."

She plopped down in the seat on the other side of me. Surprisingly, she looked put together for it to be early morning and for her to be going through so much. As always, all our hair was laid for vacation, and Imani even had gotten her lashes done. She was wearing a cute, distressed pair of jeans and a cotton cropped top.

"Imani, I'm so sorry. I didn't think it would go this far."

"I've cried all I can cry about it. I've begged him to come home. I've apologized as much as I can." She shrugged and leaned back in her seat. "I have to accept that it's over and it's my fault. I can't fight for a marriage with no foundation. It's broken and there's no fixing it. I already made the decision to sign the papers when I come back from vacation."

"Are you sure you want to do that?" I asked.

"When I look into his face, I feel so ashamed, Roze. Not only that, but I can't find his love for me anywhere in his eyes. It's over." Nobody said anything for a few beats, but suddenly she cleared her throat and focused her attention on Logan. "Is that a Gucci, Lo?"

"Yes, it is," Logan said, holding up her bag so we could get a closer look. "I thought I'd treat myself to something nice for once. Dez really hooked a sista up. Did I tell you guys that I'm having an art show at the end of the summer?"

"No, you did not. Good for you!" I said, silently clapping my hands.

"Thank you! I think it's what I need to do to get my work off the ground. And, Mani, don't hate me," Logan said, grimacing, "but it's the same weekend as your fashion show. It was the only time the venue had available."

"I'm not mad at you for finally following your heart. But I am mad that I won't be able to be there." Imani checked the time on her phone. "We should be boarding soon. Did anybody find out anything on where we're going?"

"Nope," Logan and I said in unison.

"And we're going anyway?"

"Yup," we said in unison again.

"And neither of you thinks this is crazy?"

"You know I thought about it. What if Mena was lying and she was trying to lure us to some random island?" Logan said.

"But why would she do that?" I asked. "Plus, you guys read Dez's text. It sounded just like her. Plus, Mena couldn't fake all of the photos and videos she had of the two of them together."

"It's still crazy," Imani said.

Before I could say anything else, we were called to start boarding the plane. We were the first to get on the plane and got comfortable in our cabin. Once everyone was boarded and the door to the plane closed, it got real for me.

"We're on the way, Dez," I said, looking out the window into the sky.

Keep an open mind and you'll have a good time. . . .

Chapter 35

Logan

I really loved to travel, but plane rides were never my favorite thing. Especially traveling overseas. It was like, by the time I finally got comfortable enough to go to sleep, boom! We arrived at our destination. And that time was no different. I felt like my eyes had only been closed for a few minutes when I felt a gentle hand shaking my shoulder.

"Wake up, Lo. We just landed," Roze said.

I stretched wide and sat up groggily. Once I came completely back to my body, I looked out of the window of the aircraft. The bright sun shone in on me, and my eyes fell on the beautiful surrounding waters.

The moment we were able to, the three of us got off of the plane. We made our way through the hustling and bustling travelers to get our luggage. Once we had all of it, it was time to find our resort. I pulled up the itinerary that was sent to our emails and found that we would be staying at a resort called Wonderland. We walked around for what seemed like forever trying to find where the transportation was to it in the airport. Finally, I gave up and decided to ask one of the workers. He was a stout man with a mustache and was pushing an empty wheelchair.

"Excuse me," I said, showing him the itinerary on my phone. "Where can I find Wonderland Resorts?"

He looked at it for a second and then looked around. He then looked at the email again and scratched his head. The end result was him shrugging his shoulders and walking away. I groaned and asked another worker, hopeful that time they would be able to point me in the right direction. However, that was wishful thinking. Imani and Roze weren't having any better luck. Nobody seemed to have heard of Wonderland Resorts. Just as I was beginning to think Dez might have been mistaken about where we were supposed to be staying, a throat cleared behind us. We turned around to see a middle-aged olive-colored man with a full beard standing there. He was wearing a dapper suit and holding a sign with our names on it.

"Excuse me, might you ladies be Imani, Roze, and Logan?" he asked, pointing at his sign.

"Umm . . ." Imani made a face and looked at us in a "what should we do" fashion.

"Who wants to know?" Roze asked.

"I do apologize for approaching like this. My name is Alejandro, and I was hired to drive you to the Wonderland Resort."

"Uh-huh, and how do we know you're not just trying to lure us somewhere to trade us for sex trafficking?" I asked, not trusting a word he said. To my surprise, he chuckled.

"Desiree said you might be skeptical of me, just like she was. She told me to show you this." Alejandro pulled out a folded photo from his pocket.

He held it out and showed it to us. My tension eased when I saw that it was a picture of him and Dez smiling. She had snapped a photo of them while he was driving. As usual she was beautiful as ever. Flawless. Imani, Roze, and I exchanged a look. The photo was confirmation that she had really been there.

"I really liked her," Alejandro said, smiling. "She contacted me many months ago and said she was planning a trip for her friends. She said she only trusted me to transport her friends. Where is Desiree anyway? I would love to see her."

It almost broke my heart watching him look around with hopeful eyes and a smile frozen on his face. He didn't know.

"Alejandro, Dez . . . she passed away," I told him and watched the smile on his face fade away briefly.

"Oh. I'm sorry to hear that," he said sadly. "She was a good lady."

"She was."

There was a pause before Alejandro cleared his throat and straightened up. "No matter. I'm still in charge of getting you to where you need to be. Come, follow me."

He took off walking in one direction, and I looked at my friends to see what they wanted to do. Imani shrugged and gathered her things to follow him. Roze and I did the same. Alejandro took us outside to a red SUV and helped us load our luggage in the trunk. Once we were safely inside of the back seat of the vehicle, he got in the driver's seat and drove away.

It didn't take long for me to let my guard down slightly. From where I sat, I took in all the beautiful green scenery. I smiled and waved at the people we drove past and just basked in the ambiance of being on vacation.

"Is this your first time?" Alejandro asked, looking at us in the rearview mirror.

"To the Wonderland Resort? Yes," I answered, and I saw a sly smile come across his face.

"You will have a great time. As long as you keep an open mind."

"Is Wonderland another name for Fantasy Island?" Imani blurted out.

"Ahhh, Fantasy Island," he said blissfully. "What a wonderful place. As I said, keep an open mind and you'll have a good time."

I was still so busy sightseeing that I didn't even notice that he didn't answer her question.

"Is there a reason we couldn't find any information about Fantasy Island on the internet?" Imani kept the questions coming.

"Some places are so sacred that they will never be known to the general public. You have to be personally invited."

"Ohhh, like a secret club," Roze said. "I like exclusivity. It makes me feel famous."

"Shut up," I giggled.

For the rest of the ride, we listened to Alejandro sing songs we didn't understand and even tried to sing along. I was happy that the trip was starting off on a good foot. And things got even better when we arrived at the resort. It was huge, elegant, and right off the beach. Alejandro pulled right up to the front doors and helped us unload. He was even kind enough to walk us inside all the way to the front desk.

"Alejandro! Good to see you," a young woman said with a bright smile when she saw him.

"Good afternoon, Clarissa. This is Imani, Logan, and Roze. They'll be staying in the Fantasy suite. So if you'll please, take very good care of them."

An excited glimmer flickered in Clarissa's eyes as they combed over my friends and me. After a few moments, she gave an approving nod and turned her attention to her computer screen. After a few taps, her face lit up.

"All right, I have them right here. Imani Patrick, Roze Henderson, and Logan Jamison?"

"That's us," I said.

"All right. All I need to see are your IDs, and we can get you all checked in." She turned to Alejandro and gave him another smile. "I can handle it from here."

"Great. I'll see you ladies in seven days," he said and started to walk away.

"Wait," I said, making a face. "I thought you were our transportation while we're here."

"Trust me, you won't even be thinking about me until it's time to go," he said over his shoulder and laughed deeply.

"Oookay," I said and turned back to Clarissa.

We gave her our IDs so that she could check us in. When she was done, she gave them back to us and I was expecting her to hand us our room key. Instead, she came from behind the counter and motioned for us to follow her.

"Where are we going?" Roze asked as we walked closely behind her.

"To the Fantasy suite," Clarissa said.

We followed her down many long hallways in the large resort until we hit a wall in the back of it. It was far away from everything else and well out of eye reach of any guest or worker. I was confused as to why Clarissa was just staring at the wall.

"Um, what's going on?" I finally asked.

"Anyone staying in the Fantasy suites is very exclusive. And exclusive guests get exclusive entrances."

Before I could say another word, she lifted what I thought to be a thermostat and revealed a red button underneath it. She pressed the button once, and the wall in front of us separated. It was an entrance to a hallway giving access to a whole different part of the resort. The ground was made of marble. But not just any marble. There were the prettiest seashells embedded in it. At the end of the hallway was an elevator. We stepped through the entrance in awe.

"Follow this hallway to the elevator. You three will be staying in Fantasy suite number 3 for the next two days. Madam Freya will be to your room to see you later this evening. Please enjoy your own private pool and entrance to the beach in the meantime."

"Wait, aren't you coming?"

"I have to get back to the front desk, but don't worry. You will be very well taken care of. Your journey to your most intimate selves has just begun."

She pressed the button again, and the entrance closed. We were left standing alone in the hallway. It just was all so bizarre that it was hard for me to wrap my head around it.

"What just happened?" Roze asked, reading my mind.

"I think we're supposed to go to the elevator," Imani said.

"So you don't find it strange that there was an entrance in the middle of a freaking wall?" Roze's eyes were wide, and Imani shrugged.

"I think it's kind of cool that they're going through all this trouble to make their guests feel special. Now come on. I want to see what this suite looks like!"

She pulled her luggage behind her and went toward the elevators at the end of the hall. I wasn't able to fight my curiosity, and I quickly went after her with my luggage in tow. What *was* this place really? I couldn't help but feel that there was something else to it. And why had Clarissa said that we would only be in the suite for two days? The only way to find out was to go up.

We piled inside the elevator doors that opened first and were silent the whole way up. But even though no words were said, I could hear their thoughts just by looking at their faces. Imani was probably hoping we didn't get kidnapped, and Roze was second-guessing her decision to come. Me on the other hand? Curiosity had me by the skirt tail. Once the elevator let us off, I all but ran to Fantasy suite 3. It was at the end of the hall, and when we got inside, I was blown away. The high ceilings, the granite floors with the matching countertops, and the elegant decor had me at hello, okay? Not to mention the ocean view and the stairway from the balcony that led right to the beach.

"We only get to stay here for two days? *This* could be the vacation to me!" I exclaimed, looking around.

"There are only two bedrooms," Imani noted, tugging her luggage behind her.

"So? You act like we've never piled up in the same bed before." I made a face at her.

The two of them explored the room some more, and I put my things in one of the bedrooms. Next, I made my way to the kitchen. All that traveling had my stomach rumbling, especially since the last thing I'd eaten was the nasty meal on the plane. Okay, it wasn't nasty, but the portion size was. It was more like a snack. I opened the fridge and groaned when the only thing stocked inside was yogurt and fruit. I wanted some real food. I looked around for the room service pamphlet. Right when I found it and was about to call down and order some hot wings, there was a knock on the door.

"Who is it?" I called since I was the closest to it.

"Madam Freya, dear," a sweet voice called back. "Clarissa should have told you I was coming."

I peered through the peephole and saw a short woman who had her hair up in a bun. She looked nice and harmless, but still I cautiously opened the door. She was wearing scrubs and had a cart with her. She saw me looking skeptically at the cart and laughed.

"Everyone gives me that look when I come knocking. Even the ones who know what to expect. May I come in?"

"I guess," I said and stepped out of her way.

She pulled the cart inside and parked it in the living room area. Imani and Roze had come out to see what was going on. They eyed the items on the cart just like I did. They looked like what a nurse would bring into the room during testing. STD testing.

"What's all this stuff for?" Imani asked, pointing at the swab sticks.

"I'd be pleased to inform you. Everyone sit down," Madam Freya instructed and sat on a chair. The three of us sat on the couch diagonal from her, and when we were comfortable, she handed us each a cup. "For your exam, I'm going to need a urine sample from each of you. Don't worry, your names are already on your cups and—"

"Wait, exam? What the hell!" I exclaimed.

"Yeah, what do we need an exam for?" Roze asked, making a bewildered face.

"In order for you ladies to be granted access to Fantasy Island, you must consent to sexually transmitted disease testing. We also do a mouth swab and a finger poke for the rapid HIV test. Here, read these."

She handed each of us a pamphlet, and the first thing I noticed was the naked couple under the words "Fantasy Island" on the front. Fascinated, I opened it up and read more. It described in limited detail what Fantasy Island was. Basically it said that it was a place to live out your ultimate truth. Highlighted inside were the Fantasy packages.

"'Mandingo, Euphoria, Lover's Lane, and Build Your Own,'" Roze said, reading out loud. "These are the Fantasy packages?"

"Yes. I assume that you sent over your bio sheets a while back?"

"Yes, our friend told us that we needed to," Imani answered with a nod.

"Perfect. Then when you get there, your counselor will help sort you into whichever package best fits your needs. But first, we need to get your testing out of the way."

"What do you mean I can't go to Fantasy Island?" The shout from the hallway was so loud that it sounded like it was coming from inside of the room.

Roze, Imani, and I jumped up to go see what was happening while Madam Freya just shook her head. Roze yanked the door open just in time to see two men wearing the same kind of scrubs as Madam Freya escorting a woman out of a room. She was a pretty Latina woman and fiery. She was swatting the men's hands away every time they tried to grab her.

"I paid twenty thousand dollars to come here, and now you're saying that I can't even go? Assholes!"

"Jasmine, we are sorry, but you knew the rules. Just because you aren't having a herpes outbreak right now doesn't mean we can't detect it in your blood. We can't allow you on the island."

"I can't believe this shit!" Jasmine cried out, and when she saw us staring, she reached out to us. "Take me with you! Please! Please! I have to go. I *have* to! This is a once-in-a-lifetime experience. And I have to! I just have to!"

Madam Freya gently wedged her way in between us and shut the door so we couldn't see what was going on in the hallway. Still, I'd seen all I needed to see. So had Roze and Imani. We all made a beeline for the bathroom to pee in our cups. Whatever Jasmine so drastically wanted to experience, I just *had* to see. And it wasn't like I hadn't ever gotten an STD test before.

After we peed in the cups and gave them to Madam Freya, she swabbed our mouths, took our blood work, and did a finger poke. All of our HIV tests came back negative, but we had to wait two days for the other results. In the meantime, Madam Freya told us to enjoy the resort.

When she was gone, the three of us disappeared into one of the rooms. Imani connected her phone to the TV, and I called room service to order our food. After I hung up the phone, I dug into one of my suitcases and rummaged around until my hand wrapped around what it was looking for. When I pulled out the liquor along with three shot glasses and showed them to my friends, I had a big smile on my face.

"Looooo!" they groaned, seeing the 1942 bottle.

"Oh, yes I did, for old times' sake," I said and climbed into the bed with them.

"That nasty-ass shit!" Roze pretended to throw up.

"Well, I guess it's fitting for the occasion," Imani said and pointed at the TV. "This was in my email this morning."

On the screen was the PowerPoint that Dez had made us on our last vacation together. Imani pressed play, and I felt all of the emotions watching it just like I had for the first time. Everything from the music to the media was the same. The only thing that was different was the ending. Instead of saying, Cheers to our last trip together, it said, Thank you for being the best friends I could ever ask for and for traveling the world with me. Cheers to all of your new adventures. I'll be with you always. I love you forever.

My chest felt heavy reading those words because they were true. Dez was gone, but lately I'd been feeling her presence all around. The three of us held each other tightly, and I was surprised to see that none of us cried. Maybe we were learning how to transfer our sadness into happiness. Happiness because we'd gotten to experience such a phenomenal woman. One who wasn't selfish, and one who sent us her love from the grave. Not many could say they ever had or ever would come close to even touching something so precious.

"Oh, Dez," Roze whispered and let her head fall on my shoulder.

"She has one last gift to give us," Imani said, smiling at the frozen screen. "I say we accept it and let our girl rest in peace. What y'all think?"

"Agreed." Roze nodded.

"It's going to be hard, but I'm there with you," I said.

Dez deserved eternal peace. She'd spent a big chunk of her life being our problem solver, and now it was time for us to be that for ourselves. I wasn't sure what was in store for us when we returned to our homes, but that could be pushed to the side for a week at least. I opened the 1942 bottle and poured each of us a shot. Once we all had them, we held them in the air.

"To Dez," Imani cheered.

"To Dez," Roze concurred.

"To . . . Fantasy Island!"

We threw back the shots, not complaining about the burning sensation in our chests. Imani pressed play on the television again, and we welcomed the sound of TLC's "What About Your Friends" in our ears one more time.

To be continued . . .